"I'm begging you, Macey."

"Oh, now we might be getting somewhere. Derek McConnell begging…" She considered. "No. Sorry. I thought for a moment there that the idea of Mr. Perfection on his knees might be interesting, but I'm afraid it doesn't move me after all."

"Then what does move you, Macey? What will it take to persuade you?" His voice was low and husky.

That's what he sounds like in bed.

Her mouth went dry. With distaste, she told herself—but she knew better.

Leigh Michaels has always been a writer, composing dreadful poetry when she was just four years old and dictating it to her long-suffering older sister. She started writing romance in her teens and burned six full manuscripts before submitting her work to a publisher. Now, with more than sixty-five novels to her credit, she also teaches romance writing seminars at universities, writers' conferences and on the Internet.

Leigh loves to hear from readers. You may contact her at P.O. Box 935, Ottumwa, Iowa 52501, U.S.A. or visit her Web site: leigh@leighmichaels.com

Books by Leigh Michaels

HARLEQUIN ROMANCE®
3720—BRIDE BY DESIGN
3731—MAYBE MARRIED
3748—THE MARRIAGE MARKET
3759—THE BILLIONAIRE BID

THE BRIDE ASSIGNMENT
Leigh Michaels

HARLEQUIN®

TORONTO • NEW YORK • LONDON
AMSTERDAM • PARIS • SYDNEY • HAMBURG
STOCKHOLM • ATHENS • TOKYO • MILAN • MADRID
PRAGUE • WARSAW • BUDAPEST • AUCKLAND

ISBN 0-373-03772-4

THE BRIDE ASSIGNMENT

First North American Publication 2003.

Copyright © 2003 by Leigh Michaels.

CHAPTER ONE

THE woman sitting across the desk from Macey looked nervous. No, Macey thought, worse than nervous. She looked terrified.

"I've tried everything," the woman said. "Though I don't suppose I should tell you that. If you knew how many places I've applied for a job and been turned down, you wouldn't want to hire me either." She bit her lip.

Macey smiled. "Well, I'm looking for a little different sort of person than many personnel managers are," she said, deliberately keeping her voice low and soothing. "As a matter of fact, Ellen, we find that women like you are our best workers."

"Really?" Ellen's voice was little more than a squeak.

"Oh, yes. We love hiring women who are returning to the job market after taking a few years off to raise children. As a rule, women like you are highly motivated, you're realistic, and you have excellent time management skills."

Ellen sighed. "Looking for a job has certainly made me realistic. And the divorce has given me all kinds of motivation. I don't know about time management."

"Any woman who's raising a couple of kids has learned how to balance at least six tasks at the same time."

Ellen smiled faintly. "I guess you're right about that. Do you have kids? You sound as if you know."

Macey kept her voice light. "Only observation, not personal experience."

"Sorry," Ellen said under her breath. "I guess I shouldn't have asked that."

"There's nothing wrong with asking questions. We encourage it around here. When we send you out on a temporary job, it will be important for you to know what questions to ask so you can get the work done."

"I see." Ellen sounded doubtful.

Macey didn't push the point. "Of course, there's also a downside for women in your position—your skills are a bit rusty and you're not really sure what you want to do with the rest of your working years."

Ellen relaxed. "Yes. That's it exactly. And some of those jobs sounded so complicated—"

"That you were afraid of getting in over your head, and so perhaps you didn't interview very well. That's why I think you'll find temporary work is a good choice, for now. You won't have to face any more interviews after today, and you'll be able to try out all sorts of different jobs."

"But if I can't do the work—"

"We won't send you out until you've had some refresher courses and practice, and we'll choose your first jobs very carefully. Trust me, Ellen—our biggest problem here at Peterson Temps is that just when we get an employee completely trained and comfortable so she can handle anything a new office throws at her, she finds a niche she really likes, the company hires her full-time, and we're left shorthanded again."

Ellen smiled. "I guess that's lucky for me. At least you have an opening."

"Let's get you started with the official paperwork." Macey pushed back her chair and led the way to the reception room. "Louise, please review the personnel handbook with Ellen and then take her over to the skills lab for an evaluation.''

Ellen said, ''You mean like a test.''

''Not really. Just a checkup so we can see where you'll need practice and extra training.''

The receptionist pulled a booklet from a drawer. ''Macey, Mr. Peterson left word for you to see him as soon as you're free.''

''Thanks, Louise.'' Macey held out a hand to her newest employee. ''Don't hesitate to come and talk to me at any time, Ellen.'' She crossed the waiting room, tapped on the closed door of her boss's office, and pushed it open without waiting for an answer. ''Robert? You wanted me?''

Too late to retreat, she saw that there was a second man in the office, sitting across the desk from Robert Peterson. He turned halfway around at the sound of her voice, as if he was annoyed by the interruption.

Why hadn't Louise warned her? ''I'm sorry,'' Macey said. ''I didn't realize you weren't alone.'' She started to back out of the room.

But Robert beckoned her in. ''My visitor is the reason I asked for you. Come and sit down, Macey. This is Derek McConnell. Derek, my office manager, Macey Phillips.''

McConnell…the name didn't ring bells. Was he a new client, perhaps? Though it was a bit unusual for someone who wanted to hire temporary help to actually come to the office; most of their business was developed through word of mouth as one employer told another about everything Peterson Temps could do. And in most cases, the actual requests came not in person but by phone, often with no time to spare for the niceties. *We need a receptionist for a week while the regular one is out with the flu. We need an executive secretary so ours can go on vacation. We need a financial analyst to handle a one-time project.*

Or perhaps Derek McConnell was on the other end of the equation—he, like Ellen, might be a worker seeking a job. Though he didn't seem to fit the part, Macey thought as he stood up to greet her. There was something about him which spoke of power—and he was giving her an appraising look, almost as if she was being subjected to some sort of test. Not at all the sort of survey she was used to getting from people who were applying for work.

She returned the look, studying him just as closely. He was tall and broad-shouldered, obviously an athlete despite the perfectly tailored navy pinstriped suit he wore. His hair was brown but liberally threaded with gold, which glimmered in the sunlight falling through the office window and made him look like a wayward angel. His eyes were brown as well, framed with lashes which in Macey's opinion were far too long, dark, and curly to be wasted on any man. She'd gotten only a glimpse of his profile, when she'd first walked in and he'd turned halfway 'round, but even a glance had been enough to show that it, too, was flawless.

In short, in all the obvious ways in which the world judged men, he was Mr. Perfection.

And there's not the least doubt that he knows it, she thought. She stretched out her hand. "My pleasure, Mr. McConnell. What can I do for you?"

Derek McConnell didn't answer right away. He waited for her to take her chair before he sat down. Then he propped his elbows on the arms of his chair, tented his hands together, and said, "Ms. Phillips, I want you to find me a wife."

*   *   *

For an instant, Macey Phillips looked as startled as if he'd kicked her in the kneecap. Then she gave a little gurgle of a laugh that Derek thought sounded almost like a low-pitched set of wind chimes.

"Well, that's one we don't hear too often," she said. She looked toward Robert, obviously expecting him to share the joke. Derek watched a small line form between her brows as she realized that Robert apparently didn't see the same humor in the situation that she had. She looked back at Derek. "I'm afraid I don't quite understand. You must realize that Peterson Temps isn't a matchmaker, or a dating service."

"I'm perfectly aware of that. If I wanted a dating service, I'd consult one. I very deliberately chose to come here instead."

She frowned. "You want to hire a temp?"

"Not exactly. Perhaps it would be easiest if I started from the beginning, Ms. Phillips. If you have time, that is."

"Oh, yes, please." She leaned forward. "And of course I have time—I couldn't turn my back on this story right now any more than I can walk out of a movie halfway through."

She was laughing at him. Irritating as that was, it was also comforting in an odd sort of way. At least it appeared that Robert was right about her—this woman wouldn't take any crazy notions of trying to marry him herself. Now if she'd just get serious enough about his problem to actually help him...

"My father is George McConnell," he began. "You would probably be more likely to recognize his nickname—"

"You mean the founder of the Kingdom of Kid? The one who made it possible for a child to turn thirteen in this country without ever having slept in, crawled over, climbed on, eaten, or played with anything that wasn't produced by a McConnell company? That George McConnell?''

He was startled. ''As a matter of fact, yes.''

''So if he's the king, that's why they call you the crown prince of the Kingdom of Kid.''

Robert cleared his throat reprovingly. ''That's nothing more than a tasteless reference by a popular magazine which is only trying to increase its circulation.''

Macey glanced at him and then back at Derek. ''Sorry,'' she said. ''I'm all ears. Really.''

Derek's gaze wandered for just an instant, coming to rest on the small, almost pointed ear that peeked out from under the gleam of her dark brown hair. It would have been a nice ear, if she'd been wearing a tasteful single pearl in the lobe instead of a chunk of something that looked like broken pottery. And there was only one piece of pottery, he noted. The other earlobe, tiny and elegantly shaped, was bare. ''My official title is vice president of operations.''

''Same thing,'' she said, almost under her breath.

''Not quite. My father has reached the age when he'd like to—'' He caught himself in the nick of time; he'd almost said *abdicate*. Damn her royal references, anyway. ''He's planning to retire. But the members of the board of directors, he tells me, are a little itchy at the idea of making me the new CEO.''

''They probably still think of you as the kid whose picture is on the baby food jars and toy packages.''

''That doesn't help matters, but it isn't the crux of the problem.''

Her eyes widened. ''I was joking. You mean it really *is* you on all those labels and boxes?''

"An updated version of an old photograph," Derek said stiffly. How absolutely stupid it was to feel defensive about it.

"I see. That explains why you need a wife—so they'll take you seriously."

"Not exactly. They're quite aware I've grown up."

"Yes—partly because of that magazine we were talking about. You know, your directors have a point. You're not only thirtyish and unmarried, but you have quite a reputation as a man about town. Naming a single and childless playboy as the CEO of a company specializing in kids would be something like hiring a guy who's violently allergic to cats and dogs to manufacture pet food."

Robert said, "Or a vegetarian to run the sausage factory."

Derek jumped. He'd almost forgotten the man was still there. "I can understand that it might cause some consternation on Wall Street, yes. That's why I'm here."

Macey said, "Because you want to hire someone to pretend to be your wife, just until you're established in your new job? That shouldn't be too—"

"No."

She frowned. "You've lost me, Mr. McConnell. Which part of that did I get wrong?"

"Most of it." He held up one hand and ticked off his points on his fingertips. "No hiring. No pretending. No temporary arrangement."

Her jaw dropped. He had to restrain himself from reaching over and nudging her chin back into place. She had a cute mouth, actually, but it was distracting when it was hanging open that way. Almost as distracting as that single kooky earring. Where had she found it, anyway? On some archaelogical dig?

Derek forced himself to look at her eyes instead. "It's

not as if I have any objections to the idea of marriage. As a matter of fact, intellectually I agree with the board of directors that image is important and a married man would make a better CEO for a company like this one.''

''So what's the problem?''

''The problem is, my father's sudden wish to retire has caught me unprepared. I have to act soon, but right now, I don't have the kind of time it would take to find the right woman. And you see, I have to be certain she is the right woman.''

Macey nodded slowly. ''Because a *divorced* childless playboy as CEO of a company specializing in kids would be even worse than a never-married one.'' She rubbed her temples. She looked as if her head hurt.

Derek shrugged. ''If I'm going to do this at all, I might as well do it right. It's time for a new picture on the baby food jars, anyway.''

She stared at him, her eyes widening as she took in what he'd said. ''You're not serious. You expect this wife to have your kids?''

''It's just part of the deal. As long as we agree to the details up front, I don't see any reason for her to object—and I certainly don't understand why you should get your toenails twisted, Ms. Phillips. Considering what I'm offering, there will be no shortage of interested women.''

He watched as her dainty white teeth closed hard on her lower lip. There was no doubt in his mind about what she would have liked to say—he could almost see the words she was trying so hard to swallow.

He conceded that the statement had probably sounded a bit egotistical. But that didn't make what he'd said any less true. And since when was it conceited for a man to recognize and admit that he was considered to be a prize?

He watched her gaze flicker; she was apparently ticking

through a card file in her brain, considering possibilities. Finally she shook her head. "I can't think of anyone in our agency who would even consider the idea, Mr. McConnell. I think a dating service might well be a more logical—"

"I didn't seriously expect you to have a list of workers categorized under the heading *Prospective Wife*. The kind of woman I intend to marry isn't going to be working for a temp agency anyway."

"All kinds of people work for temp agencies," she said coolly. "For all kinds of reasons."

"Sorry. I didn't mean that the way it sounded."

She looked as if she doubted it. "Never mind. The point is, I'm afraid you've lost me, Mr. McConnell. You said you wanted us to find you a wife. Now you're saying you don't think we can. What exactly are you looking for?"

"Someone who will consider all the possible candidates, winnow through them, and select a few finalists for me to choose from."

She was still looking at him as if he were two blocks short of an alphabet, but the professional calm was back in her voice. "Well, that makes a little more sense. You want to employ a personal assistant who has human resources experience and familiarity with hiring. Maybe someone with a little psychological training thrown in. Do you prefer to work with a male or female?"

Robert leaned forward. "We've already concluded that a woman would be better for the job. Making this kind of judgment seems to require a feminine eye."

Macey didn't miss a beat. "Well, let me think about the people who are on our employment rolls right now. We have a number of good personal assistant types, but I'll have to check on the details. Can I get back to you in a day or two?"

Robert said, "Macey will take care of you, Derek."

She shook her head. "Don't make promises lightly, Robert—it won't be easy to find someone to fit the bill. Are there any other restrictions, Mr. McConnell? Would you prefer a motherly sort to choose your bride, or a younger woman who would have more direct experience with the sorts of concerns you have?"

"Macey," Robert repeated, enunciating each word carefully, "will take care of you, Derek. She'll get your problem solved—*personally.*"

Macey had bit her bottom lip so often and so hard during this conversation that it was starting to feel permanently indented. But the idea that Robert wanted to stick *her* with this job was the ultimate; she simply couldn't swallow any more. She took a deep breath and stood up. "Mr. McConnell, if you'll excuse us for a moment, Robert and I need to have a short conference. Alone."

Was that amusement she saw flickering in those big brown eyes? But he politely said, "Of course. I'll just wait outside."

She held her tongue until the door had closed behind him and then spun around to face her boss. "Robert, you can't saddle me with this!"

"It's an opportunity we can't turn down, Macey. Think of the business that young man will be able to throw our way. We could open another branch office. Just think of the goodwill we'll earn when you succeed."

"Think of the disaster when I don't!"

"Macey, stop and think. How hard can it be? Honestly, my dear—how difficult can it possibly be to find a woman who wants to marry young Mr. McConnell?"

Considering what I'm offering, there will be no short-age of interested women, Derek McConnell had boasted.

The damnable thing was that he was probably right. That mix of arrogance and power acted as an aphrodisiac for a lot of women. Even if he hadn't been the crown prince of the Kingdom of Kid, even if he hadn't had a dollar to his name, there would still be women swooning over Derek McConnell.

The fools.

No, finding willing women wouldn't be the problem. But Robert was missing the point. Derek McConnell had said *the right woman*—and that was the part that wasn't going to be easy. A man who was Mr. Perfection himself wouldn't settle for less in the woman he married.

"Robert, the man's delusional." Macey knew she sounded desperate, but she didn't care. "If he thinks he can just buy himself a crate of happily-ever-after—"

Robert shook his head. "Oh, I don't think that's what he believes at all. You know, Macey, it's really the wild-eyed romantics who are the delusional ones, believing in love at first sight and all that sort of garbage. Derek feels that the odds of having a successful marriage are a lot better if one chooses carefully—uses one's good sense instead of relying on instinct and hormones and luck."

"So let him use his own good sense instead of trying to hire someone else's!"

"Under the circumstances, it seems to me to be smart to seek an outside opinion. Derek seems to me to be a very levelheaded young man. He just doesn't have time for—"

"And you think I do have time? Come on, Robert— you know how busy I am. Why don't you hire some sensible grandmotherly type? Somebody who would make it her top priority to find someone who can make him happy?" *Instead of someone like me, who doesn't care*

*who he marries as long as the choice doesn't come back
to haunt me?*

"Because you're all those things you rattled off a little
while ago, Macey. You have human resource and personnel experience and a psychology background. And you're
a young woman who can understand the additional
stresses on a marriage today."

"Because I've been married," she said slowly.

"And—forgive me—because you're so obviously not
interested in being married again," Robert said. "That
fact will give you a certain perspective, an extra measure
of distance so you can see the situation clearly. Most people would get caught up in the romance of the whole
thing. Your grandmotherly type—even if she existed—
certainly would."

"You're quite right that you don't need to worry about
me getting romantic over this," Macey said dryly.

"Exactly my point." He made a shooing motion toward the door. "Now, run along before Derek gets impatient and thinks we're not interested anymore."

"I couldn't be so lucky," Macey muttered.

She was right; Derek McConnell hadn't given up. He
was sitting next to Louise's desk, paging through a magazine. He was apparently oblivious to the admiring looks
he was getting from Ellen, who was eyeing him over the
edge of the personnel handbook she was supposed to be
reviewing.

He stood when Macey came out of Robert's office.
"Who won the argument?" he asked with obvious interest.

Macey looked through him. "It wasn't an argument. It
was a professional discussion. And can we please con-
tinue this in my office instead of in public?"

"That means you lost."

"No, that means I don't have a great deal of time free today."

"Robert warned me about that." He consulted his wristwatch. "I've got a busy schedule too, you know, but I blocked out two hours to deal with this, and you've already used up one of them."

"That's certainly efficient. You're devoting two whole hours to settle a matter that you'll be living with for a lifetime."

"No, I'm devoting two hours to bring you up to speed so *you* can settle it. Though I admit to having second thoughts about turning over my future to a woman who can't hang on to both of her earrings."

Macey's hand went automatically to her earlobe. "Oh. I pulled one off this morning because the phone was making my ear hurt, and then I forgot to put it back on."

"The dinner plate you were wearing is what made your ear hurt. It's hardly fair to blame it on the phone." He paused just inside her office door and looked back at her, one eyebrow raised. "You did invite me in, I recall. I presume you have some questions?"

Macey gritted her teeth. She closed the door on Ellen's avid interest and Louise's more tactful but no less eager curiosity, sat down at her desk, and pulled out a fresh notepad and a new pencil. "Perhaps you'll give me some parameters that will help narrow the search. Of course, I'll start by noting that anyone wearing funky earrings need not apply. Obviously you would interpret a difference of opinion regarding her jewelry as indicating a serious character flaw in a woman, and we certainly can't have that."

"Since I'm the one who'd have to actually look at the jewelry, I think I'm allowed to have a say in it," he pointed out. "You can't see your own earrings, so that's why you're not even sure if you're wearing both of them. It's everyone else in the room who gets an eyeful. Though the size those things are, I don't understand how you can walk around and not notice that you're lopsided.''

Macey looked for her second earring, found it stashed in the pen tray of her desk drawer, and very deliberately threaded the post through her earlobe. ''There. Perhaps you'll be less cranky now that I'm not lopsided anymore.'' *But I'm not counting on it.* ''What else?''

''I haven't exactly made a list.''

''You amaze me. She doesn't have to be a natural blonde, five-feet-ten, size four, big blue eyes, with a doctoral degree?''

Derek settled back in his chair and looked thoughtfully past Macey and out the window. ''I hadn't thought about it, but that sounds like a good start.''

She considered stabbing him with the pencil. *No, it's not deadly enough.* ''I'm serious here.''

''All right—you can skip the doctorate. A degree of some sort would be nice, but—''

''By all means,'' she said, and wrote it down. ''For the sake of the future children's genetic heritage, she should not only be eye candy but brilliant too. Would you prefer that degree to be in math or science?''

His eyes narrowed. ''Do you get paid extra for sarcasm?''

Macey looked at him blandly. ''No, it's a fringe benefit and available only on rare jobs. Consider yourself one of the lucky few. What about hobbies? Do you want a woman who shares all your interests, or one you can escape from on the golf course?''

''It would be nice if she played golf. Maybe a little tennis, too.''

''All the comforts of the country club. And she should

be a gourmet cook, I suppose, so she can entertain all your important guests? At least, I don't imagine the board of directors eats baby food when they all get together.''

His eyes sparkled. ''You might be surprised. A few of them are old enough that's about all they can manage anymore.''

The flash of humor came and went so quickly that Macey tried to convince herself that she'd imagined it. But the gleam of laughter in those big brown eyes had left her feeling a little breathless, almost light-headed—and she certainly hadn't fantasized that.

''She doesn't need to cook,'' Derek said. ''She can hire caterers.''

Macey had to pull her attention back to the subject. *Caterers? Oh, yes, we were talking about entertaining.* ''Still, if she knows her way around a kitchen, the caterers can't take advantage of her. Do you have any pet peeves I should know about?''

''Well—I detest frivolous names. You know the kind of stupid monikers I mean—Bunny and Muffy and Taffy and Honey and—'' He paused, looking at her thoughtfully.

''Oh, don't spare my feelings,'' Macey reassured him. ''I have a very frivolous name—I've always thought so. All right. Anyone named Elizabeth, Sara, or Rachel may apply, but all others will have to legally change their names first.''

''You're right,'' he said. ''Your name does sound pretty funny. How did you come to be named Macey, anyway?''

''I was born there.''

''What?''

''In the department store. There was a big white sale going on, one day only, and my mother thought she had enough time to pick up an extra set of sheets and a few towels before she went to the hospital. She was wrong.''

He looked as if he was too stunned to speak. Macey decided she liked him better that way.

''Mom always said at least I had the good taste to be born in linens instead of pots and pans,'' she mused. ''Anyway, that's why she named me after the store, because they ended up giving her the sheets and towels. She just spelled it a little differently.''

''Good thing the white sale wasn't going on at Wal-Mart,'' he said faintly.

''Thanks—I'll add that to my list of things to be grateful for.'' Macey doodled on the notepad. ''You do realize that with this thing about names you're eliminating two-thirds of all former sorority girls? Unfortunately, ·that's the very place I was going to start looking.''

''You won't have to look. Just select.''

Macey stopped doodling. ''I'm not sure I know what you mean.''

''It's not a matter of finding this woman. I've already found her.''

She blinked twice and shook her head, trying to clear it. ''What are you talking about? If you already have a woman in mind, what do you need me for?''

''Crowd control. I know at least a hundred women who on the surface appear to be possibilities. The trick is to pick the half dozen out of those hundred who could actually make the cut, so I don't have to waste my time with the other ninety-four or so.''

''And how do you suggest I do that? Ask them to fill out applications?''

Derek shook his head. ''Too obvious. Interviews, I think.''

''Oh, I can see them lining up on the sidewalk, waiting

their turn in my office. And what would that prove, anyway? Anyone can look good on a job interview, when they know they're on trial.''

Derek frowned. ''You have a point there.''

''To judge whether they'd be right for you, I'd almost have to study them in their natural habitat. And that—''

''—is an excellent idea. Brilliant, in fact. No wonder Robert was so certain you were the woman for the job.'' He leaned back in his chair and smiled.

Macey tapped her pencil on the notepad in an attempt to buy herself a little time to figure out what was going on. Not that it mattered; she wasn't likely to understand Derek McConnell if she had an eon or two to study him. *Perish the thought.*

''We'll start tonight,'' Derek said. ''There's a cocktail party before the symphony concert. At least a dozen of my possibles should be there. I'll point them out and you can start observing.''

''I don't—''

He frowned. ''Now's where it gets tricky,'' he said. ''What's the proper etiquette, since you're working for me? Do I pick you up, or just meet you there?''

CHAPTER TWO

MACEY stared at him, trying not to believe what she'd heard. But she couldn't avoid the facts. It was quite clear to her that Mr. Perfection not only assumed she'd be attending the party, he actually thought she'd be eager to go.

"Hold it right there," she said. "I am not going out with you."

Derek looked as if she'd picked up the industrial-size stapler from her desk and slammed it over his head. "Of course you're not. Get a grip, Ms. Phillips. Going somewhere together is not the same thing as going out. This is not anywhere close to being a date."

Fury roared through Macey's veins, but she kept her voice icy calm. "For your information, Mr. McConnell, I hadn't made that mistake. I didn't assume you were inviting me to be half of a cozy little romantic duo."

"Well, I'm glad we have that all cleared up."

"But my evenings are already reserved."

From the way he suddenly sat up a little straighter, it was plain that she had gotten his attention. *Probably only because he doesn't believe I could have anything worth doing after work,* Macey thought. But at least he was taking her seriously.

"*Every* evening?"

She nodded. It was only a small exaggeration, after all.

"Then I see just one alternative."

You need to get someone else. Relief surged through her. Finding the right matchmaker was still going to be a pain, but at least she'd be rid of the major portion of this nightmare. And if Derek was to request a change, Robert could hardly argue. He might be annoyed. He might even be a bit suspicious—but he couldn't very well blame Macey simply because the client had changed his mind.

She was drawing a breath to tell him that she would buzz Robert and arrange another conference right away when Derek spoke.

"I'll tell my father that I've hired a personal assistant, and you'll run this operation right out of my office."

Macey choked.

"It won't be as efficient, I'm afraid," Derek said thoughtfully, "and I expect it'll take longer for you to meet all the women on my list, because I don't encourage them to hang around me at work."

Macey could almost feel herself turning blue from lack of air.

"Of course, in that case I couldn't pay you directly— it would look very fishy if I didn't put my personal assistant on the company payroll. So to convince my father that you're worth a paycheck, you'll have to look like a real employee, which means you'll have to do some bona fide work as well as your undercover assignment. Just to maintain appearances, you understand. But from what Robert told me about what a great worker you are, I'm sure you can handle whatever I need."

Macey finally managed to get a single wheezing breath, but the only difference it made was that she started to cough.

"And it might cause some problems around here, too," Derek mused. "Of course, since this is a temp agency, surely it won't be any trouble for Robert to find someone to fill in for you as office manager for a few weeks."

"A few *weeks*?"

"I suppose you'd be taking a risk that Robert would like the new person better and you'd come back to find your job gone—but then you might also decide you like working for me. If we got along well enough, I might even keep you on."

Talk about a fate worse than death.

Derek looked very directly at her. "Unless you'd rather rethink the matter from the beginning, of course."

If she'd built the box herself, Macey admitted, she couldn't have made it fit any tighter.

He lounged back in his chair. "You're absolutely certain that every single one of your evenings is spoken for?"

"Perhaps not *every* one." Macey felt a little hoarse.

"Good. Then let me ask you again. Shall I pick you up tonight, or meet you at Symphony Hall?"

The moment Macey stepped into the town house, the scent of roasted garlic greeted her, and she knew Clara had had a better-than-usual day. With a sigh of mingled relief and gratitude, Macey hung up her coat and went into the kitchen.

Clara was stirring a big pot on the stove. Her gray hair was askew, looking almost as if it hadn't been combed today. But she was wearing a burgundy slacks set instead of the sweatsuits she favored on her off days, and she had even put on a dash of makeup.

Macey gave her a hug. "Something smells wonderful."

"Potato soup. It's a new recipe—I got it from one of the ladies at ceramics. There's lemonade in the refrigerator if you'd like some."

Macey poured herself a glass and leaned against the counter. "You went to class today?"

Clara nodded. "I got the second coat of glaze on the

wise men so they can be fired again, and I cleaned the shepherds and a couple of the animals. I think the whole nativity set will be done in time for Christmas.''

''That's great, Clara.'' Not that Macey really cared when—or even if—it was finished. But having a project gave Clara a reason to get up in the morning and to get out of the house. ''I'm glad you went.'' Macey sipped her lemonade. ''Clara—I have to go out for a bit tonight.''

For a moment, she thought Clara wasn't going to answer at all, and her heart sank. It took so little sometimes, even on a good day, to throw Clara into the depths again.

But finally the woman said, ''Where are you going?''

Just my luck, Macey thought. *The one time I wish she wouldn't take an interest in the outside world, she's going to want the details.* ''It's something to do with the city orchestra. I'm afraid I have to hurry—I need to be at Symphony Hall by seven.''

''Then it's a good thing the soup is ready.'' Clara gave the pot a final stir and reached for a ladle, frowning a little. ''Why so early? The concert doesn't start till eight-thirty.''

Macey winced. How on earth did Clara happen to know that?

Clara glanced at her and answered the unasked question. ''There was a story in the newspaper this morning, all about the soloist. It sounds like it'll be a very good program. You'll have to tell me all about it.''

''Well, I'm not sure I'll actually be going to the concert, just this thing beforehand.''

''What thing? You mean the fund-raising cocktail party?'' Clara put the ladle down. ''Macey, that's what the story was mainly about. That party costs two hundred dollars a ticket. I didn't know you were so fond of the symphony.''

Trust Derek McConnell to leave out a few minor details.

"Actually," Macey admitted, "I'm...well, I'm meeting someone there."

"Meeting someone?" Clara said slowly. "You mean like a date?"

Macey's heart dropped. *Now we're in for it.*

"Macey, you've actually got a date? With a man?"

"Honey, this is so far from being a date it isn't even on the same continent."

Clara looked at her more closely. "You're blushing as if it's a date."

"It's not a date, all right?" Macey heard the sharpness in her voice and took a deep breath, trying to calm herself. "It's work."

"I thought you had an ironclad agreement with Robert that you don't work nights or weekends."

Macey bit her lip.

"You thought I didn't know about that," Clara mused as she dished up a second bowl of soup. "It's not that I don't appreciate it, you staying at home to keep me company, to help keep the black clouds away. But with this new medicine, I really am getting better, Macey. And in any case it's well past time for you to come back to life."

"You are my life, Clara."

"And I've been selfish enough and sick enough to let you think that, and act as if it were true. But it's three years now since Jack died. You're a young woman. He wouldn't have wanted you to mourn him forever."

Just what I don't need tonight, Macey thought. *Reverse guilt—my husband's aunt giving me a hard time for not leaving him in the past.*

"We'll talk about it later," she said hastily.

Clara didn't bring it up again, but the subject hung in

the air between them. With relief Macey finished her soup and went to get dressed.

Perhaps it was fortunate, she thought, that she didn't have many choices, so she couldn't drive herself crazy wondering what was appropriate to wear to an upper-crust cocktail party. The only disadvantage was that she had absolutely no excuse for being fashionably late, because it took no time at all to select her forest-green business suit. It was the dressiest thing she owned, it was almost new, and it fit well. It was even stylishly cut, compared to most of her wardrobe—which fit solidly into the business-basics category.

Nevertheless, when she was dressed, she looked into the full-length mirror in her bathroom and surveyed the suit and the coordinating pinstriped blouse with a flicker of distaste.

She sighed and started to dig in her closet, emerging finally with an ivory silk camisole, all but strapless and covered with delicate embroidery, to substitute for her tailored blouse. She couldn't even remember where it had come from. A long-forgotten lingerie party given by a friend, perhaps.

Now if she could just get out of the town house without Clara commenting about her running around in something that looked like underwear… She put the long jacket back on and buttoned it all the way up.

Clara inspected her without a word and said a calm good-night. But as Macey pulled the front door shut behind her, she thought she heard Clara mutter, "It sure *looks* like it's a date."

Macey paid off her cab outside Symphony Hall and got a receipt to add to her expense account. Tucking it into her tiny evening bag, she stopped just inside the main entrance. There were people all over, and they—unlike her—obviously knew where they were going.

A man spoke behind her. "Excuse me."

Macey felt herself flush. "Oh, I'm sorry. I didn't realize I was blocking traffic. It's just that I'm not sure where the cocktail party's being held."

"Then I'm your man." He held out an arm with a ceremonial flourish. "My name's Ira Branson. And you are—?"

By the time Macey had introduced herself, they were nearing a wide arched doorway which led into what looked like a ballroom. A man who resembled a cartoon caricature of a butler was standing at the door, his posture so stiff that for a moment Macey wasn't certain whether he was real or a wooden statue wearing white tie and tails.

Ira pulled a strip of red paper from his pocket and the butler-figure looked disdainfully at it before he took it carefully between two fingertips. Then he turned a narrowed gaze on Macey.

Macey said, "I'm sorry, I don't actually have a ticket, I—"

The doorman put his head back so he could look down his nose at an even more precipitous angle. "Madam, this is not the sort of occasion where we sell tickets at the door to anyone who happens to have the price of admission."

Fine with me, Macey wanted to say. *Because—as a matter of fact—I don't have an extra two hundred bucks on me this week.*

"Now come on, Wilson," Ira protested.

The doorman ignored him. "This event is open only to those who have been specifically invited."

From somewhere inside the room, Derek McConnell materialized beside the butler. "Wilson, my dear jerk, you can knock off the grandiose act and stop insulting my guest.'' He pulled a ticket from his breast pocket and flourished it under the man's nose. ''She doesn't have a ticket because I'm holding it.''

The doorman's gaze flickered. ''Your guest? Very well, sir. If you say so.'' Doubt dripped from his voice.

''I'm *so* pleased to meet you, Wilson,'' Macey murmured. She was tempted to give the man a friendly punch in the arm, or maybe offer a high-five, but she didn't want to be responsible for causing him to have a stroke.

The doorman ignored her and managed to look even more like a stone-faced statue.

Ira stuck out his hand to Derek. ''McConnell—good to see you again. I didn't mean to barge in on your territory, buddy, but Marcie here was a bit lost—''

''Macey,'' Derek corrected. ''Her name's Macey.''

''Oh. Sorry. As I was saying—''

''Thanks for bringing her in,'' Derek said, and drew Macey away from the entrance. ''It's about time you got here.''

She headed automatically for a secluded corner. ''Was it really necessary to be rude to Ira?''

''You're worried about his feelings? He couldn't even get your name right.''

''At least he made sure I got to the right place.''

''Hey, it's not my fault you were late. I waited around out in the hall for you till people started looking at me oddly.''

''Including the guard at the door, I imagine. I'll bet if you had greased his palm with an extra hundred he might have found me slightly more palatable.''

''Well, you have only yourself to blame for the reception you got. I offered to pick you up.''

''And you think walking in beside you would have

made him any more impressed with my style? You know, Derek—'' Though they'd agreed to use first names, it was the first time she'd actually done it. His name felt funny on her tongue, as if she'd taken a bite from the jelly dish expecting it to be sweet, only to taste jalapeno peppers instead. ''That's the man who should be vetting your choices.''

''Wilson? You're joking.''

''Dead serious. He obviously already knows everybody who's anybody—to say nothing of who isn't. I'll bet by the end of the evening he'd have a short list all ready for you. And after all, why should choosing you a wife take any longer than selecting a new Miss America? The requirements are so similar. I'll go ask him to take over, if you like.''

''Have a drink instead—you'll feel better. I'd recommend you stick with the wine. It's not the best vintage, but at least it's not watered down like the Scotch is.''

''Two hundred bucks a ticket and they water the booze?''

Derek shrugged. ''It leaves a little extra for the symphony that way.'' He waved down a waiter. ''White or red?''

''White, please.'' Macey took the glass he handed her and looked across the room.

It was swarming with people, young and old, all of whom obviously knew each other. She watched a matched set of blondes air-kissing near the hors d'oeuvre table. Derek had said something about a dozen possibilities attending tonight, but it looked to Macey as if the crowd included more like fifty women of the right age and pedigree.

She smothered a sigh. ''Anyway, now that I'm actually

in, you don't have to hover over me. Just point out the most likely candidates and I'll get to work."

"I'll take you around and introduce you to them."

She eyed him over the rim of her glass. "You're not serious. Bad enough they may have already seen you talking to me."

"How? We're standing in a corner behind a pillar."

"Trust me. If they're interested in you at all, they know exactly where you're standing and who you're with."

"If that's the case, I can't see that it'll hurt anything if I introduce you."

"You can't really think these women will show their true colors with you standing right there. Are you completely illiterate about the way women think, or what?"

"They're sure as heck not going to confide in a total stranger."

"You might be surprised at what they'd do. But in fact I don't expect them to. I'm not going to sidle up to each one and ask her to whisper in my ear what she really, truly thinks of you. Even if I didn't die of boredom from listening to the platitudes, it would be completely useless."

"So what are you going to do?"

Excellent question. But in fact, Macey reminded herself, she didn't have to become best friends with every woman in the place, she only needed to get a feel for the sort of people they were. And she didn't have to make the final choice. All she really had to do was eliminate the obviously impossible—like the bottle redhead who was standing next to the bar, almost wrapped around a man in an effort to keep herself upright.

The woman must have had a head start to be drunk already, Macey thought. Especially if Derek was right about the purposely weak drinks being served at the party.

Macey didn't doubt it a bit, because he'd certainly been correct about the wine. She couldn't imagine forcing enough of it down to even get a buzz, much less lose her inhibitions.

Which was something of a shame, actually, for this job would be a whole lot more fun if her mind was just fuzzy enough around the edges not to remember tomorrow exactly what she'd done in the name of finding Derek McConnell a bride.

At any rate, the redhead was definitely out. It might be a slow beginning, but at least she was on the road.

One down. Forty-nine—give or take—to go. And that's just tonight's crop.

"Hold this," she said, handing Derek her wine. She unbuttoned her suit jacket and slipped it off, folding it over her arm. "See you later."

"Don't you want your—" He held out the stemmed glass.

She shook her head. "Just pretend you don't know me, all right?" she said, and plunged into the crowd.

Derek swore under his breath. *Pretend you don't know me.* Well, that was just great. What was he supposed to do now? Prop himself against the pillar with a wineglass in each hand and wait while Macey made her rounds?

He'd sooner go home. He wasn't used to being treated like a coaster—nothing more than a handy place to park her drink until she decided whether she wanted it again— and he was damned sure he didn't like it. It would serve her right if she came back to report and found him gone.

Not that he dared leave, with her out there acting like a loose cannon.

Bringing her to the party at all had been a calculated risk, of course. But if she was going to check out all the women he knew, she would have to go where they congregated. He'd considered the odds and decided he could live with them, but that had been before she'd ditched him and gone off on her own.

What had happened to the woman he'd hired—the one Robert had sworn was capable, levelheaded, and completely trustworthy?

He heard a low wolf whistle nearby and looked around in surprise. Ira Branson was holding up the pillar from the opposite side and staring across the room. "If I'd had any idea what was under that jacket," he said, "I wouldn't have been so willing to let you cut me out at the door, McConnell."

Derek eyed him with distaste. "If you think it'll do you any good, go ahead and give it a shot."

"You mean you don't mind?"

Pretend you don't know me. Fine—if that was what she wanted, he could play along. "Hell, no. Just holding her ticket doesn't give me any claim."

"You mean it really was her ticket? I thought you were just picking her up. Thanks, buddy." Ira ducked between a bald guy with a paunch and a matron in maroon.

Just as well, Derek thought. With both hands full, he couldn't have given Ira the punch in the nose he deserved, anyway.

Idly, Derek watched him cross the room in the direction Macey had gone. It might be amusing to watch Ira get his comeuppance. If Macey ran true to form, the guy would probably end up standing in the opposite corner from Derek, acting like a hat stand and holding the jacket he'd been so pleased to see her shed.

A waiter came by with an empty tray so he ditched the pair of wineglasses, then turned back to survey the room. Near the hors d'oeuvre table he saw Ira on the outskirts of a group of young women. The group shifted, and Derek's jaw dropped.

He'd been too preoccupied when Macey took off her jacket to notice what was underneath, and in any case, barely a moment later she'd disappeared into the crowd. Just a couple of minutes ago, he'd been too irritated at Ira's juvenile reaction to stop to wonder why he'd been so impressed.

Now he understood.

She turned as he watched, and the overhead lights shimmered on the almost-sheer fabric, and on the fancy stitched design, and on the equally silky, nearly bare shoulders.

No wonder Ira had shot across the room like a bird dog who'd spotted a quail.

Derek caught a flash of movement from the corner of his eye just as a low feminine voice said, "The male of the species truly is a disgusting animal. Shall I get you a napkin to mop up the drool?"

He deliberately turned his back toward Macey and resumed his place against the pillar, folding his arms across his chest as he looked down at a blond woman in a yellow cocktail dress. "Hello, Dinah. How are you tonight?"

"Fine. Who's the babe?"

"How should I know?"

Dinah's big blue eyes narrowed. "Because until a few minutes ago the two of you were huddled in this corner whispering."

Huddled? That was a point for Macey, Derek admitted. *They know exactly where you're standing and who you're with,* she'd said. Apparently she'd been right.

His gaze drifted back across the room. It took him a moment to find Macey, because she wasn't where he'd expected she'd be. Instead of standing with the group of women by the hors d'oeuvre table, she was strolling across the room. With her hand on Ira Branson's arm.

"Now just a darn minute," he said.

Dinah shook her head sadly. "You really do have it bad," she murmured.

Not even close, Derek wanted to say. But if he opened his mouth, of course, it would lead to all sorts of questions he didn't want to answer.

With a careless wave, Dinah moved off toward the bar.

Dammit, Derek thought. Macey was supposed to be cozying up to the women in the room, not to Ira Branson. What in the hell did she think she was doing, anyway?

Not what you're paying her for, he told himself. But Dinah's reaction had made it clear that he could hardly go break up that twosome without causing an earthquake.

So what was he supposed to do instead? Hover in the corner watching in frustration?

It would serve her right if he took matters into his own hands. Went over her head. Made his own decision after all.

Because it was a sure bet he couldn't make a worse choice than she was likely to. If Macey Phillips's taste in men ran to a loser like Ira Branson, what kind of woman would she pick out for him?

He was damned if he'd sit around and wait to find out.

It had taken Macey less than five minutes to wipe the names of every woman in the group off her mental blackboard. Figuratively speaking, of course, since she didn't actually know any of their names—and that, she could see, was going to prove a major handicap.

Still, the elimination process had been easy enough. Of the six women standing by the hors d'oeuvre table, two were wearing wedding rings, one was sporting an enormous solitaire diamond, one waved her hands nervously whenever she spoke, one had a laugh that sounded like a tortured cat, and the last was at least ten years older than she was pretending to be.

Six women down. Sort of.

Because there were two problems. Not only did she not know exactly who she'd eliminated, but she had no idea whether they'd been on Derek's list in the first place. If he'd just been reasonable about pointing out who he wanted her to check out...

Of course she hadn't exactly helped matters by shooting off on her own, she admitted. Perhaps if she'd stuck around, explained, made her case...

She looked over her shoulder toward the pillar. All she could see beyond it was part of Derek's coat sleeve and the woman he was talking to. A very pretty blonde wearing soft creamy yellow.

No point in walking back over there as long as he was occupied with Princess Buttercup.

You're on your own, Macey.

She noticed Ira Branson hanging around the fringes of the group. He perked up the instant he saw her glance at him, and he came straight to her. "I actually thought there for a while that you were with McConnell," he confided. "Till he straightened me out."

And you're going to be on your own for a while longer, Macey. Well, she'd asked for it—telling Derek to pretend he didn't know her.

So what was she going to do? At her current rate of progress, Derek McConnell would have checked himself and his walker into a nursing home before she'd found him a wife.

But maybe Ira could help...

She laid her hand on his arm and drew him a little way from the group of women.

"You know," she said earnestly, "I was hoping you'd come over. It's so hard to meet people in a group. For one thing, they always mumble, and in a noisy crowd like this I have trouble hearing. It would make me much more comfortable if I knew people's names before I was actually introduced to them. Like that group I was just with. I think there was a Betsy and a Susan, but I wouldn't dare actually use the names for fear of being wrong."

Ira looked puzzled. "Betsy?" he said. "Susan? I don't think I know them."

Okay, Plan B flopped too—what's next?

Macey tried to be philosophical about it, but it wasn't easy—not only wasn't she making any progress, but now she'd saddled herself with Ira.

Talk about shooting yourself in the foot, Phillips.

A woman in burgundy chiffon came up to her. "I don't believe I know you," she said. "I'm with the Friends of the Symphony. Most of the people here tonight are. If you'd like to join, our membership chairman is right over there." She pointed to a woman in blue lace who was standing by the piano. "I'll introduce you, if you like."

Macey gave a casual glance to the woman in blue lace, and then looked again, longer and more thoughtfully, at the patrician face, touched with a few lines left by time and laughter.

Membership chairman, she thought. The woman would know everybody. And probably everything *about* everybody.

Macey felt as if the sun had just broken through a mass of storm clouds. "I'd love to meet her. That's a wonderful—"

Derek's hand came to rest on Macey's arm. "That's a

wonderful idea you should think very carefully about,"
he said. "Because it's not just a matter of paying dues
and carrying a membership card. Belonging to the Friends
demands lots of time and energy."

The woman in burgundy looked confused. "What are
you talking about? You know perfectly well—"

Derek had pulled Macey out of range.

She protested, "I was just starting to make progress!"

"What the hell do you think you're doing?"

"What you should have done in the beginning. I ought
to have realized right away that it's a waste of time to
talk to the young women. The matrons are always the
ones who really know what's going on. But just as I'm
about to meet the person in charge of membership, you
come barging in and make me look like some kind of nut.
Now if you want to make up for this blunder, take me
over there and introduce me to the woman in blue lace
by the piano."

"Not on your life."

Macey wanted to stamp her foot. "Why on earth not?
I'll bet you she has some pretty definite ideas who would
make a good wife for you."

"I'm not taking that bet."

"See? You've just proved my point, if you think
she..." Macey paused, suspicious. "And exactly why
not?"

"Because," Derek said grimly, "the woman in blue
lace by the piano happens to be my mother."

CHAPTER THREE

DEREK had seen the flash of temper in Macey's eyes before. A couple of times, in fact—once that afternoon in her office and again soon after she'd arrived at the party. But compared to the way she was looking at him now, those occasions had reflected nothing more than minor irritation. He braced himself for the hurricane that was about to hit.

But her voice was low and almost sweet. "And you were seriously going to stroll me 'round the room making introductions and hoping she wouldn't notice me?"

"Could we discuss this in a corner somewhere?" *Like maybe a corner of Asia—that might be far enough away.*

"Oh, it's way too late to hide behind a pillar."

"Of course, if you hadn't decided to call attention to yourself tonight by dressing up like a—" Derek caught himself a millimeter from the edge of the chasm.

"You were saying?" Macey's eyebrows arched inquisitively. "Like a…?"

"Never mind. It's done now. Fortunately the symphony's tuning up and the party's over. So let's just consider this a trial run, assess what we've learned, and start from scratch."

"I have a better idea. Let's consider it an unmitigated disaster and quit while we're ahead. Don't let me keep you from the concert." Macey turned on her heel and was gone.

Beside Derek, Ira Branson cleared his throat. "I could

have told you that would happen. You had your chance with her, McConnell, and you blew it.''

Derek had had enough. ''So now it's your turn? I notice she didn't ask you to drive her home.''

Ira frowned, working it out, and then his brow cleared. ''Probably has her own car.''

''Otherwise she'd have been begging you for a ride— I know.'' A flicker of yellow caught his eye and he turned toward Dinah, feeling irritable. ''What is it now?''

The blonde said, ''Goodness, we're touchy tonight. Your mother went on into the hall, Derek, since she'll be introducing the guest conductor. But she asked me to give you a message—she's saved a couple of seats next to hers in the front row. Shall I go let her know that since your little friend has walked out on you, one will be enough? Or are you too broken up over your spat to sit through the concert at all?''

McConnell Enterprises—informally known as the Kingdom of Kid—owned offices, warehouses, and factories scattered across the country, but the headquarters were located in a sprawling new building on the outskirts of St. Louis. In large part, it had been Derek's ideas and Derek's plans which had shaped the new building, and since the day they'd moved in, he had never approached the place without feeling a sense of accomplishment and pride.

Until this morning.

They'd built the structure solidly enough to withstand a direct hit from a tornado, but today it looked a little fuzzy to Derek, as if he was looking at it through a fog. It wasn't the weather outside that concerned him, however, but the climate inside the executive wing—and the threat it presented to his future.

His plans had all been laid out since he'd joined the firm right out of college. But even before that, when he'd worked each summer at one of the McConnell factories, it had been in the back of his mind that someday he would succeed his father. And he suspected George McConnell had been thinking about the matter earlier yet—like clear back when he'd brought home each new toy for a toddler Derek to try out.

But now it was all at risk because the directors wanted a married CEO. Their point of view might be prehistoric, shortsighted and just plain wrong, but convincing them otherwise would be no easy matter. And though the requirement was probably discriminatory in a legal sense, what was the point in filing a lawsuit? Even if he succeeded in forcing his way into the job, the working conditions would be impossible for him and threatening for the company's survival.

It wasn't as if he had any real objection to going along with the requirement, anyway. So he got married—big deal. He'd always intended to get around to it sometime.

It had been a perfectly decent plan, his sensible search for a wife—and there was no reason it should have fallen apart. If Macey just hadn't gone off like a rocket last night…

But the fact was she had, and now his plan was shot to smithereens. The trouble was the full board of directors had scheduled a formal meeting to take place in exactly two weeks, and one of the items on the agenda would be his father's planned retirement. Derek had hoped—had even expected—to use that meeting to announce his wedding date.

Now he was going to have to pick himself up and start over again, from scratch.

Well, almost from scratch. The symphony party had

accomplished one thing, at least—it had marked Dinah off his list. He supposed he had Macey to thank for that much, because she was certainly the reason Dinah had let the corrosive acid seep into her usually sweet voice. He wondered if Macey would appreciate it if he called her to express his gratitude.

His father was already in the office, leaning against the desk of their mutual secretary and reading a letter. When Derek came in, George McConnell pushed his reading glasses up on top of his head, making his thinning reddish hair stand up in a sort of rooster's comb. "Late night, son?"

Derek resisted the urge to check his wristwatch, because he knew perfectly well he was on time to the minute. "Not particularly."

George grunted. "Well, I'm glad you're here. The chairman of the board is stopping by this morning. Perhaps you'd like to sit in on the meeting? I've asked for a presentation and taste test on the new line of organic baby foods."

Macey's voice echoed in his mind. *I don't imagine the board of directors eats baby food when they all get together...* He could picture the appreciative gleam that would spring to life in her big hazel eyes when she heard this story.

But of course she wouldn't be hearing it.

"Derek?" his father said, his voice a little sharper. "Do you want to join us?"

"I—uh…"

"He said he'd like to see you…. That must be him coming down the hall now. Half an hour early, too." George McConnell let his voice sink to a whisper. "Keep him occupied for a minute, will you? I have a couple of things to finish before I can spend all day dancing attendance on him.''

The chairman of the board advanced on Derek with a toothy smile and outstretched hand, his voice booming. ''Hello, Derek! I was hoping you'd be able to sit in today. Truth is, I wondered if you'll be free this weekend. My daughter's home right now—from Stanford, you know. She's almost finished with her degree. I think the two of you will have a lot in common.''

Derek didn't let his smile slip. ''Not this weekend, I'm afraid.''

''Then just name the day. She'll be here for a while. She'll be doing an internship downtown, so she's taking advantage of the free rent at home.'' His grin grew even wider.

''I...uh...'' Derek took a deep breath. ''Well, this is a little embarrassing, sir. I can't very well....it would be a little awkward....you see, I'm...''

Okay, McConnell, make up your mind where you're going with this. I'm dying of a mysterious disease... I'm hearing the call to become a monk... I'm running off to join the Foreign Legion...

''I'm engaged to be married,'' he said.

The chairman's grin disappeared. ''First I've heard about that.''

And you're not the only one. ''I can't go into detail just now.'' Derek shot a look over his shoulder at the door of his father's office, trying his best to look like an anxious son. ''You see, I haven't had a chance to inform my parents yet, so I really shouldn't be telling anyone at all. Actually we haven't even talked to *her* parents, and you know how it is with etiquette, sir. Women insist on taking all these things in what they think is proper order.''

George McConnell came out of his office, rubbing his

hands together. ''Well, now we can get on with business. Derek, are you all right? You look pale and sweaty.''

No fooling, Dad. You should feel it from this side.

''Your mother tells me you were restless last night— not acting at all like yourself.''

''Well, you know how that goes. It was the symphony, after all—''

George frowned. ''But you *like* the symphony, Derek. She thought you weren't feeling up to par, and she wondered if you were coming down with something.''

''You know,'' Derek said heartily, ''I think she's right. And I'm awfully afraid I might be contagious. Maybe I should just go home.''

Normally, Macey liked going to work. There were days, of course, when her level of enthusiasm wasn't exactly stratospheric, but on the average she loved her job. Loved the unexpectedness of each new day. Loved the people. Loved the puzzle of putting the right worker together with each new job. Loved hearing the stories of how Peterson Temps had once more saved the day.

Not this morning. Today, she was going to have to face Robert Peterson and explain the unexplainable.

She wasn't even going to have the advantage of confessing that she'd messed up. Not that she was exactly proud of the way she'd blown last night, because she wasn't—but she wasn't about to take the blame for something that wasn't her fault. She'd tried to tell Robert that the plan was unworkable. She'd tried to tell Derek that he was nuts. She'd tried in every way she could think of to stop the train wreck from happening.

But it wasn't much satisfaction to know that she'd been absolutely right.

And she *really* wasn't looking forward to telling Robert

about how all the goodwill, along with the future business he'd hoped to win from Derek McConnell, had flown south like a flock of butterflies—because it wasn't going to migrate back again.

She dressed with extra care—though she didn't wear her best suit, the forest green one. After last night, she thought, it might be years before she could bear to put it on again. Though she often left her hair loose around her shoulders, today she put it up in a professional-looking French twist. She added a pair of chunky earrings that Clara had made in ceramics class and painted to compliment the apricot and teal tweed of her suit. And she stepped into her highest heels. She was going to need every inch of self-assurance when she faced Robert.

She'd been at her desk for an hour, shifting paper and trying to be productive, when Robert came in. She gave him a few minutes to get settled and then tapped on his door. "If I can have a minute, Robert…"

He was just picking up the telephone. "Yes, this is Peterson." He waved Macey to a chair and mouthed, "I'll be right with you."

She sat down, folding her hands primly in her lap and trying to come up with an opening line that wouldn't simply make things worse.

"Yes," Robert said and turned his chair to face the window, so his back to was to Macey. "Yes, I think…. I understand. Yes, we can do that." He wheeled around and put the telephone down.

She took a breath to begin, but Robert spoke first. "That was Derek McConnell."

Macey was stunned. The last thing she'd have expected from Derek was that he'd be a tattletale.

Oh, do grow up, Phillips, she told herself. *You sound like a second-grader.*

"I can explain, Robert. At least, I'll try to explain—though since you weren't there, you can't possibly picture what it was like last night—"

"Explain what?" Robert sounded only mildly interested. "Never mind, you can fill in the details another time. I told him you'd be right over."

"Over?" Macey asked uncertainly. "Over where?"

"Derek's apartment. He's taking a day of sick leave, he said, in order to plan what he called Stage Two. Run along, now—you don't want to keep him waiting."

Yes, I do.

"And then," Robert said comfortably, "you can tell me all about how Stage One went when you get back."

Derek didn't live in a sleek glass tower as Macey would have expected, but in a solid old block-square warehouse that had been converted into lofts. Part of a once-bustling complex that overlooked the Mississippi River, it had sat empty for years before being rescued and renovated.

It even had a uniformed doorman, who looked Macey over and said politely, "Who did you wish to see, ma'am?"

"There's no wishing about it," Macey muttered. "Sorry, it's not your fault that I'm a bit steamed. I'm here at Mr. McConnell's request."

He picked up the house phone. "I'll announce you anyway, ma'am. Who shall I say—" He paused. "A lady to see you, sir. Yes, sir, I'll send her right up." He turned back to Macey. "It's the fifth floor. The elevators are right down that hall."

She didn't remember to ask for an apartment number until she was already on the elevator, and then she decided it was too much bother to go back downstairs. As it happened, however, she didn't need a number. Derek's apartment wasn't *on* the fifth floor—it *was* the fifth floor.

He opened the door before she could even ring the bell. "You don't look sick," Macey announced.

In fact, she thought, he looked pretty good all the way around. He was wearing jeans and a dark blue pullover that emphasized the breadth of his shoulders, and he was barefoot. The casual look suited him.

"Maybe not," Derek said. "But I feel pretty sick at the moment."

"Not nearly as sick as you're going to be if you don't leave me alone. I only came today in order to get this settled once and for all. I told you last night I was done, and—"

"Macey, take it easy on me, will you? I really do have a tearing headache."

"You deserve it."

"How about sitting down over a cup of coffee and talking about it?"

"What is there to talk about?"

"Please?" He pointed to a long leather couch. It was the only place she could see to sit, except for the hardwood floor. The spike heels of Macey's shoes clicked firmly against the polished oak as she crossed the room.

Behind the couch, a wall of windows looked out over the river. The stainless steel Gateway Arch gleamed off to one side, and far below a row of barges made slow but steady progress north against the current.

She sat down and looked around. The apartment was almost entirely open, except for a big square brick core placed smack in the center and reaching all the way to the shadowy ceiling far above. From the couch she could see two sides of the core; built into one wall was a huge fireplace and an even larger television screen. Along the other visible wall, indented into the block, was a small but efficient-looking kitchen, set at an angle from the front door and separated from it by a narrow work island. Though the living room soared the full height of the loft, at one corner of the core an openwork iron staircase spiraled upward to what must be a bedroom. It occupied half of the upper reaches of the loft and was blocked off from below only by a wrought-iron railing.

Talk about your basic bachelor pad, Macey thought.

Despite the lack of furnishings, however, it didn't appear that he had recently moved in. The room didn't have the unfinished appearance of a brand-new decorating scheme. It didn't look raw; it just looked empty, as if he didn't want to be bothered with more.

Derek came back with two big mugs. "It's only fake cappuccino," he admitted. "But it's actually not bad stuff."

Macey took a tentative sip, set the cup down, and looked him straight in the eye. "You honestly have no clue how much your life is going to change if you get married," she said. She didn't intend it to be a question.

"You don't like the cappuccino."

"I didn't say that. Anyway, the cappuccino is only a detail. Any woman on that list of yours either already owns a cappuccino machine or she'll get one for a shower gift. She's also going to have a lot of other stuff."

Derek shrugged. "It's not like I've already filled the place up."

"I'm not just talking about physical baggage. The point is, instead of talking about Stage Two—whatever that involves—I think you'd be better off to give some serious thought to whether you want to do this at all."

"Of course I do."

"Of course you *don't,*" Macey said flatly. "That's why

you're trying to hire me. So you'll have someone to blame if it doesn't work out.''

"You're just trying to get out of the job.''

"Yes, I am. But I still think you shouldn't be in such a rush. Have you even considered how you're going to go about fitting a woman into your life?''

He said dryly, "There have been a few, you know.''

"I don't doubt it a bit. That just proves my point. Having an overnight guest now and then is a whole lot different from living with somebody. All right, let's leave emotional adjustment out of it for a minute and just talk about space.''

He waved a hand. "There's lots of it.''

"Open air, yes. But I'm betting this apartment doesn't have enough extra closet space for a three-year-old, much less the kind of clotheshorse you're contemplating marrying.''

He sighed. "You may have a point there. But I don't have a choice about what I do anymore.''

Macey put her head back against the soft leather couch and gave an exaggerated sigh. "And I obviously don't have a choice about whether I hear the details. What's happened now?''

"This morning, I was talking to the chairman of the board. And I...sort of...announced that I'm engaged.''

She sat up slowly. "Who's the lucky woman?'' she asked suspiciously.

"I didn't give him a name.''

Slowly, she released the breath she'd held. At least he'd maintained a shard of common sense. It could have been a great deal worse. On the other hand, if he had just blurted out a name off the top of his head, Macey would be off scot-free. It would be Derek's problem to convince the lady in question, and nothing at all to do with Macey.

Unless, of course, it had been *her* name he'd blurted out....

And why, she asked herself, would an idiotic idea like that come into her mind? Even Derek wasn't desperate enough to think of that little twist—and Macey was glad. *Very* glad. So glad, in fact, that she wasn't even going to consider the idea for an instant, for fear he might overhear her thoughts and act on the notion before he stopped to think. It would be just like him.

"So the rumors will be flying," she mused.

"I bought myself a little time by telling him I had to talk to my bride's parents before there could be an announcement."

"Talking to the bride might be a nice idea, too. You actually think he'll keep quiet about it?"

"He keeps company secrets all the time."

"That's an entirely different thing. But you know him—I don't. Maybe you'll be lucky. So what are you going to do?" she asked, keeping her voice carefully casual.

"Get engaged, of course."

"Oh, now that's a shocker. It's so original. So unexpected. So inventive... Dammit, Derek, I was talking about your plan. What's Stage Two?"

Derek propped his elbows on his knees and dropped his face into his hands. "I was hoping you'd help me figure that out."

Macey considered pouring the rest of her cappuccino over his head. "You haven't got even the shadow of an idea?"

"I wouldn't have called you if I wasn't desperate, Macey."

She released a long, tired sigh. "Tell me something I

didn't already know," she muttered. "Do you realize you have all the tact of a buzzard, McConnell?"

He sat up again and shot a look at her. "Would you rather I use my charm to get you to help me?"

"You *have* charm?"

"Ouch. I'm begging you, Macey."

"Oh, now we might be getting somewhere. Derek McConnell begging..." She considered. "No. Sorry. I thought for a minute there that the idea of Mr. Perfection on his knees might be interesting, but I'm afraid it doesn't move me after all."

"Then what does move you, Macey? What will it take to persuade you?" His voice was low and husky.

That's what he sounds like in bed. She didn't quite understand how she knew, but she was certain of it. The sudden, incredibly vivid image that came into her mind was almost more than Macey could handle. The idea of Derek begging had left her cold. But the vision of Derek persuading...convincing...seducing...

Her mouth went dry. With distaste, she told herself— but she knew better. "I'll see what I can do," Macey said. Her voice felt shaky.

Derek smiled. "That's my girl." He leaned a little closer. His hand moved along the back of the couch toward her shoulder, caressing the leather as if he were caressing skin... The nape of her neck prickled with anticipation.

A buzzer sounded, harsh in the empty air. Without hurry, Derek withdrew his hand and stood up. "Sorry, but that's the house phone and since the doorman knows quite well I'm here, I'd better answer. He wouldn't call unless..." He frowned.

Unless it's important, Macey finished. *Because he knows there's a woman up here.*

Derek crossed the expanse of gleaming oak floor toward the kitchen and picked up the phone. "What is it this time, Ted?" He winced. "All right. Thanks."

"Let me guess," Macey said. "Ten eligible women are downstairs negotiating to see who gets to audition first."

"No. It's my mother. She's on her way up carrying a bucket of chicken soup."

"That's what you get for pretending to be sick. Though it could be worse—she might have talked to the chairman of the board and be coming to grill you. I'll just…" Macey paused. "Wait a minute. It hasn't occurred to you to bribe the doorman to keep your female guests from running into each other?"

"Of course I pay him extra. Only it's called a tip, not a bribe."

"That's a matter of opinion. So why didn't he stop her in the lobby?"

"Because there's never been a doorman on the planet who could stop my mother if she wanted to go through, that's why. The best he could have done was slow her down. That's why he called—to warn me."

"He wouldn't have told her I'm here?"

"Of course not. It's a sizable tip."

"Probably not sizable enough, considering the trouble you must put him to. What now? How do I get out of here?"

"You don't. If you leave, there's no way you can miss running into her."

"The fire stairs?"

"They're right beside the elevator door, which will be opening just about—" He glanced at his watch. "Now."

The doorbell buzzed.

"Oh, this should be fun," Macey muttered.

"Upstairs," Derek ordered. "And be quiet, because sound bounces in here."

"It's never occurred to you that echoes may be an inhibiting factor for some women?" She climbed the stairs on tiptoe so the spike heels of her shoes wouldn't catch in the openwork iron steps.

The room at the top of the stairs was only half the size of the lower floor, but it was just as spare and open as the living room below. In the center of the room was a king-size bed swathed in a muted plaid bedspread in harvest colors. On either side stood a small table; each held a lamp. Atop one of the tables was a book, open and facedown as if he'd been interrupted while reading—the autobiography of a Wall Street mogul, she noted.

Near the top of the stairs, in the brick core, was a door which must lead to either a closet or a bathroom—there must be enough room in that core for both. Perhaps she'd been wrong about the amount of closet space, Macey thought idly.

The rest of the room was empty. From the railing, if she dared, she could look down onto the living room. But of course she didn't dare.

She sat down on the end of the bed and tried not to listen. But Derek had said himself that sound echoed. He had to know that she couldn't help but hear.

The door opened, and a warm, low, cultured voice said, "What's wrong, darling? You haven't been sick enough to take a day off work in at least a year."

Macey took off her shoes, setting them as quietly as she could on the hardwood floor, and lay down across the bedspread, on her back with her elbows out so she could press her fingertips against her ears to block the sound of the conversation from below.

But if listening had felt immoral, not listening felt stupid—how was she supposed to know when it was safe? When Derek came upstairs and found her lying in his bed?

Talk about asking for trouble.

She tried not to remember the way his hand had moved over the leather couch, tried not to imagine how it would feel against her skin.

She told herself it was no big deal. He'd touched her last night, after all. But that had been little more than a brush of his hand against her arm. And it had been in a crowd.

Here...alone...in his bed...

She muttered a curse and sat up.

From downstairs there was an instant's silence. "It's only from the deli," Mrs. McConnell said. "You know I don't do homemade. I hope it helps you feel better. I'm afraid I can't stay longer, but then you don't look as if you need your mommy to nurse you anyway."

"You're not going to spoon-feed me?" Derek asked lazily.

Macey thought she could hear relief in his voice. No surprise there.

"No, I have a lunch date. You don't mind if I freshen up before I go, do you?"

"Of course not, Mom."

"I'll just run upstairs for a moment then."

Macey heard footsteps crossing the room. It must be her imagination, she thought, but it sounded like the threatening tread of an army battalion.

"Uh—Mom—"

"What's the matter, Derek? I promise not to scold if your bed's not made. It's just that I much prefer a bathroom with a mirror that's actually large enough to see my whole face. I've never understood why, with all this space to work with, the builders made your downstairs powder room smaller than the lavatory on an airplane.''

She was halfway up the stairs when Macey regained control of her muscles. She twisted off the mattress, stifling a groan when her hip bumped against the hard floor, and squirmed underneath the bed just as Mrs. McConnell reached the top of the stairs.

The woman walked without hurry across the room, and Macey felt the vibration of each footstep. A moment later a door opened and closed.

Macey tried not to breathe for fear the dust under the bed would make her sneeze.

The door opened again. Footsteps once more crossed the room.

Another minute and she'll be gone. You can do it, Macey. You can hold your breath for one more minute…

But the footsteps didn't go down the stairs. A soft voice said, ''Excuse me for intruding, dear. But perhaps you'll let me give you some advice, as one woman to another. Next time you're hiding under a man's bed…'' Her voice dropped to a whisper. ''Don't forget to take your shoes.''

CHAPTER FOUR

FROM her shallow, dimly lighted niche, Macey could hear only the murmur of voices downstairs; she couldn't pick out words. But at least neither of them was yelling. That was a good sign....wasn't it?

Though she honestly couldn't imagine Derek's mother losing it enough to scream under any circumstances. Judging by her reaction to finding a woman under her son's bed, Macey thought it was fair to conclude that all of Mrs. McConnell's reprimands would be delivered with similar style and grace, plus a calm that would be absolutely deadly.

Macey lay still until she heard the click of the door closing before she cautiously started to maneuver herself out from under the bed. It was more difficult to move than she'd expected because the space was so confined.

How, she wondered, had she been able to get under there so fast when it took such concentrated effort to wiggle her way back out?

As soon as she was back on her feet, though she was still feeling a little light-headed, she walked around the end of the bed. The bedspread was rumpled where she'd been lying. And sure enough, there were her teal-colored heels in plain sight, one standing upright, the other lying on its side, precisely where she had so carefully taken them off. They looked almost like a department store display. She kicked one of them, and tried in vain to bite back a yell when the end of her toenail collided with the metal-capped spike heel.

Derek's bare feet made little sound on the iron stairs, but she heard him coming anyway. "Is she really gone?" Macey asked, suddenly suspicious. She'd heard the door close, but...

He crossed the room without a word and flung himself on the bed, face up, eyes closed, and arms outstretched. "She's gone."

"What did she say to you?" Macey asked warily.

"The usual sweet nothings. Not a word about the live dust bunny under my bed."

"So what did you say to her?"

"Nothing. You can't explain something to someone who's pretending it didn't happen."

Macey tried to brush the smudges off her jacket. "Speaking of dust bunnies, I wasn't the only one. Don't you ever mop the floor up here?"

Derek opened his eyes. "You're worried about the floor?"

"Oh, damn— Look, I snagged my jacket. There must be a loose spring under there or something."

He didn't seem to hear her. "Under the bed. You had to go hide *under the bed*. Of all the childish, shortsighted, idiotic stunts—"

"Hey, Einstein, look around and you may notice there aren't a lot of options up here. What else was I supposed to do?"

"It didn't occur to you to sit still and say, 'Hello, Mrs. McConnell'?"

"*What?*" Macey's voice was little short of a shriek. "You're the one who shoved me up and told me not to make a sound!"

"There's a point of diminishing returns, Macey. When you're inevitably going to get caught, you're better off to admit to it and take your punishment."

"Oh, that's rich. At least now I understand your philosophy on marriage—if it's inevitable, admit it and take your punishment." She tugged at the broken thread. Before it had snapped, it had pulled at the loose weave of the tweed, and the sleeve was now twisted so awkwardly it was beyond repair. "You owe me an outfit, McConnell."

He didn't move. "Send the bill to my mother."

"Oh sure. And I'll just include a note explaining that I'm the woman who was under her son's bed and I want compensation for damages to my clothes."

"She'd probably be amazed to find out that you had any on."

Macey sighed. "The only blessing in this whole thing is that she doesn't know exactly who was under the bed. If I'm really lucky, she might even assume it was Princess Buttercup."

"Princess—*who?*"

"The blonde in the yellow dress you were talking to at the party last night."

"Oh, you mean Dinah. No, I don't think Mom would believe it was her. Dinah wouldn't have gone under the bed, she'd have stripped down and hopped into it."

"Does that disqualify her from your list, or move her up higher?" Macey didn't wait for an answer. "Gee, why didn't I think of that? I wonder if I could have managed to get my clothes off fast enough to be convincing."

Derek held up his wrist. "I've got a stopwatch. Want me to time you while you practice?"

"I was being sarcastic, Derek."

"Imagine that. Macey Phillips—sarcastic!"

"I was trying to make the point that things could have been worse."

"I don't know—if she'd actually seen you between the

sheets, Mom couldn't have ignored the subject. Anyway, you might have been being sarcastic, but I wasn't." He propped himself up on one elbow. "We could have a race, if you'd like. See who can get naked first."

She turned 'round to give him a cold and disbelieving stare—one that would put him in his place. But as she looked at him lounging across the bed, she was stunned to find just how little imagination it took to picture him without jeans and shirt. To visualize him reaching up to pull her down beside him. Beneath him…

All right, she admitted. The man did absolutely drip sex appeal. A woman would have to be blind not to notice that.

And deaf, too, whispered a voice at the back of her mind. *And probably also suffering from a head cold that wiped out her sense of smell.*

But being aware of his magnetic power didn't mean that she, personally, found him irresistible. Far from it.

The best way to handle this, she told herself, was to ignore him.

"I want handicap points for the race, though," Derek went on.

Macey's good intentions went straight out the window. "For what? Why? You're wearing less than I am to start with!"

"But I'm lying down, so it would be harder for me to get out of my clothes. To say nothing of how distracting it would be to watch you."

Macey tried not to gulp at the idea of him lying there watching her undress. "This is not getting us any farther toward developing Stage Two."

"Spoilsport." He rolled off the bed and landed on his feet within inches of her, so close she could almost taste him.

She stepped back and the arch of her bare foot came down hard on the spike heel of the shoe she'd kicked in frustration. Off balance, she grabbed for the nearest support, which happened to be Derek's wrist. But she couldn't get a good enough grip to save herself, just enough to pull him down with her as she tumbled sideways onto the bed.

"You didn't have to attack me, sweetheart," he murmured. "All you had to do was ask." He shifted his weight so he wasn't quite pinning her down, and his fingertips grazed her temple, her cheek, her throat. "But now we're both going to have trouble getting out of our clothes."

Macey wasn't worried about that challenge. Another few minutes of this and her suit would have turned to ash anyway.

His lips brushed the line of her jaw, leaving a scorched trail. She watched his eyes darken.

"Don't bother trying to figure out the logistics." She planted a hand in the center of his chest and shoved, and when he pulled back she rolled out from under him and onto her feet. Picking up her stray shoes, she headed for the stairs.

By the time he followed, she was already perched on a high stool at the kitchen island, and the planning calendar she always carried was open on the counter in front of her. She didn't look up. "You have thirty seconds to get serious about Stage Two, or I'm leaving."

"You know, Macey," he murmured, "it's a good thing for you I'm not a suspicious sort of guy. Because if I was, I'd be wondering if the reason you were in such a hurry to get out of my bed was because you didn't trust yourself to stop at a kiss. Another cappuccino?"

"Not unless you mean a real one this time."

He put a large spoonful of brownish powder into a mug and filled it from an extra faucet in the kitchen sink, then sat down beside her, stirring the brew. Macey watched the steam rise from the mug. The water from that tap must be almost at the boiling point.

Just like your skin still is where he touched you.

"Your thirty seconds are almost up," she reminded. "And you can start by convincing me why I should hang around and help you work out a plan at all."

"Because your boss won't be happy with you if you don't."

She planted her elbows on the counter. "Do you realize that Robert fully expects you to throw enough temp work our way to justify opening another office?"

"Another office?" Derek sounded as if he'd suddenly had the breath knocked out of him.

"Another complete branch of Peterson Temps," she clarified. "So besides whatever fee he's charging you for this, you may as well know that he's expecting you to be paying forever."

He didn't answer.

"That's what I thought," Macey said with satisfaction. "I'll just be running along—you can stop in sometime and give Robert some story about why it didn't work out."

"How many temps does an office handle?"

"You don't seriously want to know."

"I'll see what I can manage. Robert can't ask any more than for me to try."

Macey sighed. "Well, first you'll have to manage getting married and getting named CEO. And after last night, I don't see how I could be much help."

"The problem last night was our being there together." He took the spoon out of the mug and licked it.

Macey tried not to watch the way his lips caressed the stainless steel. Tried not to think about how he might approach something which was softer and more flexible.

"We were unprepared," Derek said, "and we drew attention to ourselves."

"And whose fault is that? I asked you to quietly point out the possibilities, but no, you wanted to introduce me personally."

"My mistake. I admit it. From now on we can't let it be known that you're connected with me."

"Don't you think it's a little late for that?"

"It was only one evening. People will dismiss it as a coincidence, as long as we're not seen together again."

That means no more parties, she thought. *And I'm glad.*

"So what do we do instead?" Macey asked. "If you can get me all the information about these women, I can do a sort of statistical analysis, but I'm not sure how much good that will do."

"None. The whole reason I need you is the personal approach. Your feminine judgment. So you'll simply have to start hanging out in the same places these women do and getting to know them."

"You think they're just going to take a stranger under their wing and make we welcome? Get real, Derek. I don't belong in those places."

"You'll have to make yourself belong. You can't buy an Armani suit if you only shop at discount stores."

"Armani," she mused, and brushed a hand over the broken thread, still dangling from her sleeve. "That would make a nice replacement for my ruined tweed."

He didn't seem to be listening. "I'll make you a list. Two lists, in fact. Places to go, and people to look for. Mind if I grab some paper?" He reached for the planner.

"Not that page, it's got my grocery list on it." Macey pulled a sheet from the back and handed it to him. "So where am I shopping?"

"You can start with lunch at Arcadia, though unfortunately it's too late to go today. It's the in spot at the moment among the young women in this town, and on any given day there are going to be a dozen of them there. Then you'll be in, and you won't need me."

Macey stared at him. The man actually sounded as if he were serious. "I'm supposed to just drop in for lunch and end up best friends," she said. "Would you suggest I simply sit there and look forlorn until someone invites me over? Or shall I be direct and ask straight out if I can come and join the play group?"

"Well, I don't suggest that you sit there and read a book. Take someone with you. Hire somebody if you have to."

"Did I say you had as much tact as a buzzard does?" Macey asked sweetly. "Forget it—you're not even close to reaching the buzzard's level."

"Okay, I'm sorry. I didn't mean to imply that you don't have friends. There must be somebody you want to take to lunch." He winced. "That wasn't much better, was it?"

"No, you pretty much just recycled the insult. As a matter of fact, there is someone I'd like to invite. I'll let you know how it goes." Macey shut her planner with a snap. It would probably be smart, she told herself, to leave before she told him exactly what she thought of his plan. But she couldn't quite suppress the urge to have the last word. "Amazing," she murmured. "I'd have sworn you said just a little while ago that you didn't have any ideas at all about how to approach Stage Two."

Derek opened the door with a flourish. "I didn't, a few minutes ago. Isn't it incredible how sharing a bed with you inspired me?"

Macey had read the food critic's column about Arcadia when the restaurant first opened, and she'd concluded that the review was probably the closest she'd ever get to the trendy new bistro. Not that she wouldn't like to see the place. What attracted her, however, was neither the food nor the upscale clientele. She just wanted to see what a professionally run con game looked like, and she thought Arcadia was the best anywhere around.

"People don't eat at Arcadia," she told Clara as they walked from the parking ramp across the street to the sprawling building which housed the restaurant. "They *graze.*"

Clara frowned. "Like cows?"

"Something like that. There's no menu, so you don't order. You choose from a selection of food laid out on a big horseshoe-shaped table."

Clara shrugged. "Sounds like a buffet to me. Or a smorgasbord. What's so original about that? For that matter, what's so wrong with it?"

"Nothing at all. That's what makes it ingenious. You promise an unlimited choice and quantity of food, but you promote it to a clientele who survives on diet colas and lettuce. The women come to be seen, they pay an incredible price for lunch, and then they eat two carrots and a slice of cucumber. The rest is profit. It's like counterfeiting money, only it's completely legal."

Clara balked at the door. "So if it's ruinously expensive, why are we here?"

A young woman in a very tight sweater bumped into Clara's capacious handbag, almost knocking her off balance. Instead of apologizing, she rolled her eyes and ostentatiously walked around them.

Well, honey, Macey thought, *if it were my list we were checking out, you'd be off it right now.*

"Lunch is like getting a bonus," she said vaguely.

Clara's eyes widened. "You're kidding. *Robert's* paying for this?"

"No. A client I'm working for." Macey approached the maître d's stand. "Reservation for Phillips, please."

The maître d' looked pained at the idea of a diner so anonymous that she had to give her name, but he led them to a table. "Would you like to look at a wine list, madame?"

"Certainly," Macey said.

"Is this the same client you met for the symphony party?" Clara asked.

Macey nodded curtly and pretended to read the wine list. If she didn't volunteer anything, maybe Clara would let the matter drop.

"He likes your work that much?"

Macey looked over the edge of the burgundy leather folder. "Clara, I don't believe I ever said whether this client was male or female."

"You didn't," Clara said, and smiled. "But you have now, because if it was a woman you'd have answered the question instead of dodging it." She sat back in her chair with an air of contentment and looked across at the array of food. "So those are the choices of the day? Well, they won't make much money on me, because I plan to taste everything."

Macey put the wine list down and surveyed the buffet table. Though it was enormous, it was dwarfed by the sheer size of the room. There was only one dining room at Arcadia, and the tables were arranged so each one had maximum visibility. As the reviewer had said, what point was there in paying a fortune to be seen at the trendiest place in town if you ended up sitting in a spot so isolated that no one knew you were there?

"I doubt it tastes as good as it looks," Macey warned. "For all I know, the chocolate cheesecake is really made of plastic. If my suspicions are right, nobody's ever actually tried a slice, so it might as well be fake."

Not that Macey particularly cared whether the food was good. She hoped it was, for Clara's sake. But Macey hadn't come to eat, only to observe. If Derek wanted to pay the price of admission, she'd happily people-watch at Arcadia.

Because that was all she could accomplish, really. His notion that all she had to do was show up in order to be taken to the collective bosom of the young women of his social set fell somewhere on the scale between peculiar and ludicrous. What she could do was watch and listen, try to put names with faces, and get an idea of how the women on his list behaved when there wasn't a man around to impress.

Or at least, when the man in question wasn't Derek—because there were a few men in the crowd. She watched one crossing the room with a plate so fully loaded that he couldn't actually walk; he was shuffling along like a snail in an effort to keep everything level. Maybe Arcadia didn't turn quite such a marvelous profit as she'd thought....

And though Derek had been right about the number of young women milling around the buffet, table-hopping, and striking poses to impress the onlookers, there were plenty of people who didn't fit into that category too.

Clara nudged her and pointed to a table, just two rows away, where four matrons were already at the dessert stage. "It looks like you're wrong about the chocolate cheesecake. I have an idea—let's start with dessert and work our way backward through the main courses and appetizers."

Macey wasn't listening. One of the matrons at the table was the woman who had approached her at the symphony cocktail party—the one who had offered to introduce her to Derek's mother.

And right across the table from her was Mrs. McConnell. Right where she could hardly avoid staring straight in Macey's direction. And, possibly, wondering where she might have encountered her before...

That's only your guilty conscience talking, Macey told herself. There was no reason Derek's mother should recognize her. If she'd gotten a look at the symphony party, it could only have been a brief one. And there was no reason for her to notice one young woman more or less in Arcadia's dining room.

So why, every time Macey darted a look in her direction, did Mrs. McConnell seem to be watching her?

Macey chose only a few samples from the main courses to nibble on, more to keep up appearances than because she felt like eating. With Mrs. McConnell just across the room, the last thing she needed was to drip tomato sauce down the front of her dress.

But Clara made good on her threat to focus on dessert. "It's actually very nice, the way they've cut everything into bite-size pieces," she said as she finished a square inch of carrot cake and moved on to the black forest torte. "You can try them all. It's so disappointing to get a whole slab of something and then discover it doesn't taste as good as it looks. Raspberry mousse—this looks good. So tell me, Macey. You're obviously not here to eat, so I'd like to know what kind of secret operation I'm providing the cover for.''

Macey was startled.

"I know—the old, depressed Clara wouldn't have noticed," Clara said. "Of course, the old, depressed Clara would have stayed home altogether. I told you I'm feeling better on this new medicine." She shook her head at the rest of the raspberry mousse and moved on to the key lime pie.

"It's a sort of research project," Macey said. "Observing the young women. It would help if I knew their names, but I suppose even a description will help him figure out which is which."

"You don't seem to be doing much looking."

"Well, I can't exactly stare. It's rude—and it draws attention."

Clara's fork was suspended over her dessert plate. "What exactly are you observing?"

"Their behavior, their attitudes. Why?"

"Because I can stare all I like. Nobody pays attention to one old lady more or less—we're almost expected to be rude. The blonde by the buffet table, for instance..."

Macey took a quick look. "Oh, that's just Buttercup. She doesn't count—at least, she's not on the list. But what do you think of the two women she's with?"

Clara looked for a long moment. "Not much to distinguish them—from each other or anyone else."

Macey sighed. "That's the problem. They all run together, somehow."

A shadow fell across the table. "I don't mean to intrude," said Mrs. McConnell. "But I'm almost certain I recognize you."

Macey's breath froze in her throat. Very slowly, she turned to face Derek's mother.

However, the woman wasn't looking at Macey, but at Clara. "You're very familiar," she mused. "And yet…"

"Oh, that's because unlike some of our contemporaries I haven't gone in for face-lifts and skin peels and hair dye," Clara said comfortably. "And I see you haven't much either, Enid—but a bit of age looks good on you."

"Clara! I thought—"

"That I was long dead? Lots of people got that idea. This is my niece, by the way."

"Your sister's daughter?" Enid McConnell offered her hand. "Or your brother's?"

Macey tried to will herself not to tremble as she took it. She shook her head, but her voice didn't seem to work anymore.

"Macey is my brother's son's wife, actually," Clara explained. "It sounds pretty complicated, I'm afraid."

"Oh, yes. I'd forgotten for a moment, Clara, that you had just the one brother. How nice to meet you, Mrs. Phillips. I love your earrings."

Macey's hand went automatically to her earlobe as she tried to remember what she'd put on this morning. Oh yes—the ones Derek had called dinner plates.

"I made them in my ceramics class," Clara said. "But I'm getting a bit bored with it. I think when I'm finished making Macey's nativity set I'm going to try porcelain painting."

"Do sit down," Macey managed to say finally.

"Go spend some time with your friends, dear," Clara said placidly. "Enid will keep me company for a few minutes—won't you?"

Run along and play, Clara might as well have said. What was she thinking? Worse, what was she likely to say? But Macey was in no position to argue about it. All she could do was hope that since Clara didn't know her client's name, and Mrs. McConnell hadn't seemed to recognize her, that they would have no reason to compare notes.

It wasn't much comfort. Still in shock, she managed to get herself to the buffet table.

Buttercup—no, the woman's name was Dinah, Macey reminded herself—and her two friends were hovering over the salad bar as if their selections were as important as partitioning a nation. Dinah moved aside barely an inch and said, "Well, if it isn't the mystery woman. You're turning up everywhere these days. Tell me, are you new in town or just an upstart?"

One of the young women squeaked as if in protest. The other tried to hide a smile.

"Oh, I wouldn't want to ruin all the fun you're having speculating," Macey said gently. She put a strawberry on her plate and moved toward the dessert section—as far as she could get from the trio.

Well, Phillips, that wasn't a very successful investigative move.

She glanced back at the table. Clara and Enid McConnell were practically nose to nose. Macey sighed and decided to wander around the room as if she were admiring the art on the walls. If she dawdled beside each table, maybe she could overhear enough of a conversation to pick up some names, at least.

When she looked back a few minutes later, she was stunned to see that their table was empty. A busboy was gathering up the wineglasses and Clara's dessert plate.

"The ladies who were here," Macey said. "Did you see where they went?"

The busboy shrugged. "Sorry, ma'am."

Macey hurried toward the door. Even the maître d' was gone. Perhaps they'd stepped outside for some air, because it was feeling stuffy in the building—or was that only because she felt so flustered?

She paused just outside the door. As a cool breeze lifted the tendrils of hair around her face, a hand closed on her arm and pulled her aside, behind a huge concrete planter full of decorative grasses.

"Derek," she gasped. "What are you doing here? And why are you acting like a spy?"

"Because I just saw my mother come out of there."

"So you hung around to see what would happen next? That's brilliant. Was she with anyone?"

"No. Why? What happened?"

So wherever Clara was, she was alone. "Nothing much. This is impossible, Derek. They're all interchangeable anyway. Why don't you just tack all the names up on a wall and start tossing darts? If the first one you hit isn't gullible enough to take you, you can just keep on throwing till you get lucky. Look, I'll tell you the details later— the little there is to report—but right now I've lost track of my…someone…and I really need to go." She didn't wait for an answer but headed back into the restaurant.

Clara was standing just inside the foyer, swinging her handbag. "Ladies' room," she explained. "I thought you saw me leave. That was incredible, Macey."

"The ladies' room, or lunch in general?"

"No, dear. You're a smart girl, wandering around that way—giving me the excuse to ask Enid about everyone you strolled past." She unclasped her handbag and pulled out the wine list from their table. Her voice dropped to a conspiratorial whisper. "I've got the scoop on every one of them, right here."

Enid McConnell was unusually solicitous, which was enough to send Derek's suspicion meter well into the danger zone. "I'm so glad you're feeling enough better to come to dinner," she cooed as he fixed her a drink from the cart in the McConnells' living room. "I hope you're up to eating spicy things—your father's bringing home Mexican."

"I'll risk it. What's the occasion, anyway?"

"No occasion. Can't I invite my son to dinner without having an excuse? Thank you, dear." She took a long sip of her Scotch and soda. "So much better than the stuff we served at the symphony party, don't you think? I wonder if that's what gave you the funny bug yesterday... Why didn't you introduce me to that young woman, by the way?"

Well, it hadn't taken long for her to come to the point. "Which young woman?"

"You know perfectly well which one I'm talking about. The only young woman there that I didn't already know."

That was a distinction he hadn't considered before.

"I saw her again at Arcadia today," Enid said. "She was having lunch."

Treat it casually. "I didn't realize you hung out there." He dropped a couple of ice cubes in a glass for himself and put in a splash of Scotch.

"It turns out," Enid said without looking at him, "that she's the niece of an old friend of mine."

No wonder Macey had been so distracted when he'd showed up outside Arcadia. But why hadn't she told him she'd actually been introduced to his mother? Unless she hadn't. *I've lost track of my...someone...* Her words came back to him.

And he'd thought she'd been nervous because she didn't want to tell him that the person she'd taken to lunch was a guy. As if he'd have cared!

But maybe she hadn't been part of the old friends'

meeting. Maybe there hadn't been an official introduction after all. Or maybe she'd known all along that there was a relationship between his mother and this relative of Macey's....

"Whose niece?" he asked, trying to sound casual. "Anybody I know?"

"I doubt it. An old school friend. And to be absolutely accurate, she's not the niece."

Derek's head was throbbing again. "I thought you said—"

Enid shrugged. "Oh, it ends up being the same thing. She's my friend's nephew's wife."

Married? Macey was *married?*

Derek's glass slipped out of his fingers and shattered on the flagstone floor.

CHAPTER FIVE

DEREK looked down at the wreckage of the cocktail glass, but he didn't see it. He was picturing Macey.

As a long-confirmed single man, it had become second nature to him to glance at the left hand of every woman he met. It was such an ingrained habit, in fact, that he couldn't even recall for certain whether or not he'd checked Macey's. Surely he had—and yet under the circumstances in which he'd met her, perhaps for once he hadn't paid any attention.

Focused on his own marital status, it might not have occurred to him to check hers. There was no reason to, after all—he had simply accepted Robert's assurance that Macey was safe, that she was not at all the sort of woman who would get carried away by the romantic notion of marrying him herself...

No wonder Robert was so certain, dummy.

But he could see her in his mind as clearly as if they were still sitting together in Robert's office, with Derek explaining his situation and Macey listening intently—and wearing only one earring. He'd certainly noticed that. How could he have missed a wedding band?

He hadn't missed it because she didn't wear one. That was the only explanation.

Lots of professional women don't, McConnell.

Not that it mattered, of course. Ring or no ring, married or not—it didn't make any difference.

He didn't quite see why Robert hadn't told him exactly why Macey was no risk. It wasn't as if being married was a sin, for heaven's sake. But he supposed that was Robert's business, and maybe Derek just hadn't given him the chance to go into detail.

He also didn't quite understand why Macey hadn't ever mentioned it. But then perhaps he'd been so focused on his own plans that he hadn't given her an opening.

Or maybe he just hadn't been listening closely enough. All that rigmarole she'd gone through yesterday about how much his life would change if he got married... He'd thought it was just the usual feminine diatribe, but he supposed it could have originated in personal experience.

No wonder she'd said at first that her evenings weren't free....

Still, the whole question wasn't important. It was only the unexpectedness of the announcement that had shocked him, and the fact that the information had come from his mother, of all people.

He'd been startled. That was all.

Enid's voice was wistful. "That is a Waterford crystal glass, Derek."

Derek looked ruefully down at the mess. "I think you mean it used to be, Mom." He stooped to begin picking up the shards.

The wine list Clara had lifted from Arcadia was covered with her small, cramped writing. It took a couple of long and patient hours for Macey to decipher all the names and cryptic references, and then more time for Clara to recall and expand on what she'd meant by each of the notes.

"There's one where you just wrote *self*," Macey pointed out. "Does that mean self-centered, self-conscious... What else could it be? Self-possessed? Maybe selfless?"

Clara looked thoughtful. "I'm trying to remember. But

it wasn't *selfless,* that's for sure. None of those young ladies got that sort of rating. Of course, the selfless sort is more likely to be working in a soup kitchen than having lunch at Arcadia, so the deck was stacked from the beginning.''

You can't buy an Armani suit if you only shop at discount stores, Derek had said. There was some truth to that philosophy, Macey thought. A marriage was much more likely to be successful if the partners had similar backgrounds and similar expectations. And since there was no doubt whatsoever that Derek was an Armani suit kind of guy, of course he was looking for the same sort of woman.

And Macey supposed that working from his original list made sense, too. If he was going to get married in a hurry, it was more reasonable to select one of the women he was already acquainted with than to court disaster by choosing someone he knew absolutely nothing about. The odds were better—or at least they looked better.

It was just that in Macey's opinion, the women on his list were beginning to look as if they'd come from a flea market instead of a designer's workshop.

But that wasn't her problem, she reminded herself. All she had to do was cut his list down to manageable proportions. She would eliminate the obviously ineligible and leave the rest to him.

It was not part of her job to suggest that he might be wise to at least window-shop before he actually made a purchase.

"Now I remember," Clara said triumphantly. "*Self-aware.* That was what Enid called her."

"Is that good or bad?"

"The kind who can't walk past a mirror without checking herself out."

"Bad." Macey crossed off the name. "That's the very last one you got the scoop on."

They'd made a considerable dent in the list Derek had given her. In fact, Macey noted, there were only six names left on it—and wasn't that the goal he'd set originally? Her mission, he had said, was to pare his list of a hundred or so down to the half dozen most likely possibilities, and he would take it from there.

Thanks to Clara's talent for picking Enid McConnell's brain, Macey was done. Finished. It was almost like magic—all she had to do now was hand over the list and she could wrap up the entire problem of Derek McConnell.

That conclusion called for a big wave of relief, and Macey was surprised when she didn't feel it surge over her immediately. Of course, she still had to deliver the list, and probably Derek would want her to explain—maybe even justify—why each of those particular women was still in the running while the others were not. That wouldn't be fun. But when that discussion was over, she would feel light as a feather.

So the sooner she got it over with the better. She'd already wasted the better part of three days on this job, and her work was stacking up at the office. If she presented her conclusions to Derek tonight, her life would be back to normal in the morning.

And *normal* couldn't come soon enough for her.

The last thing Derek expected to see, when he strolled into the lobby of the converted warehouse, was Macey sitting on the high desk at the doorman's station, a slice of pizza in her hand and the box open beside her, flirting with Ted the doorman.

Though perhaps it wasn't quite fair to say she was flirting, just listening with ultra-flattering attention while Ted talked. He was saying something about the classes he was taking, and Macey didn't even look over her shoulder as Derek came in. He was standing beside her before she noticed him at all, and even then it was probably only because Ted stopped talking in midsentence and jumped up to greet him.

Finally she turned 'round and smiled. "How was dinner?"

"Very spicy. What are you doing here?"

"Waiting for you. Ted thought you'd be home early, so I decided to hang around for a while in the hope he was right. I have a list for you."

List? Oh, the finalists. "I thought you said you didn't find out much."

"I hadn't checked all my other resources yet when I talked to you this afternoon."

"Resources like my mother? What the devil were you thinking of?"

"Mostly," Macey said crisply, "I was thinking about how I could escape. Do you want this list or not?"

Ted was looking interested, Derek noted. "Come on upstairs."

She wriggled a bit. He wasn't sure if she was trying to get down off the desk or she was just uncomfortable at the idea of being alone with him again. But he'd already said more in front of the doorman than he'd intended to.

Unceremoniously Derek put both hands on her waist and swung her down. She was so little and light that he could have thrown her over his shoulder and carried her...but he'd already done the caveman act yesterday, he reminded himself. She hadn't made a fuss, but she'd very efficiently freed herself. If he tried it again, she'd probably slug him.

"Enjoy the rest of the pizza, Ted," she called as they reached the elevator.

"Thanks for bringing it, Ms. Phillips."

"You brought a pizza for Ted?"

"Not exactly. I was hungry and I thought you might be too."

"Sorry I wasn't home. Pizza sounds good." Derek unlocked the door of the loft and turned the lights on.

"You can relax about your mother, by the way," Macey said. "Clara—my aunt—doesn't know it's you I'm working for. And your mother didn't recognize me."

"Don't bet on it. She knows you were at the symphony party."

"She does?" She sounded as if she was short of breath.

Derek nodded. "She just doesn't know it was you under the bed. Want a brandy? Or would you like some leftover chicken soup?"

"No, thanks. Here." She held out a sheet of paper.

He glanced at it. There were six names—and one of them, he supposed, would turn out to be the future Mrs. Derek McConnell. Well, he'd deal with that a little later. He set the page on the kitchen counter and anchored it with the salt shaker. "I'm sorry about earlier."

Macey said slowly, "What are you talking about?"

Women always made themselves out to be so damned subtle, he thought, and yet they insisted on having every single detail spelled out. They seemed to especially like dwelling on the ones that were most embarrassing for the guy they were talking to. "Wrestling you around on the bed. Things like that."

"Oh. Of course."

She sounded wary. No, Derek thought in disbelief, she sounded like she'd honestly had no idea what he was referring to. As if the incident had been so unimportant to her it had been instantly dismissed from her mind. But one thing was sure—he was in too deep now to back out without finishing. "I shouldn't have done that."

"That's right—you shouldn't have," she said crisply. "Thanks for the apology. Do you want me to go over the list with you?"

"Dammit, Macey, why didn't you tell me you're married?"

"Why on earth should I?" Her voice was sharp. "Is that why you apologized? Because you're afraid of finding an irate husband on your doorstep wanting satisfaction? I thought better of you than that, Derek."

If she thought he had apologized just to save himself from a punch in the jaw... Derek gritted his teeth. He'd like to see the guy try—but he didn't suppose it would be too smart to tell Macey that. "Throw that little fact in, and it's no wonder you didn't want my mother to find you under my bed."

Her eyes narrowed. "That was low."

"So was calling me a coward."

She knew it, too—that was obvious from the way she looked away. She said, more softly, "I wasn't aware that my marital status had any bearing on the job."

"Well, of course it doesn't," he said, feeling awkward. "It just... Well, it would have been better if I'd known."

"Better how?"

"Because it would have been a perfect setup. A married woman whose husband is too busy to accompany her needs an escort sometimes—like to the symphony party. I'd have just been doing you a little favor. Heck, we could have gone anywhere together without causing comment."

Her eyes widened. She was looking at him as if he were one mattress short of a bunk bed—for no reason that he could see. What had he said that she thought was so far off track, anyway? "Are you really that naive, Derek?"

"It happens all the time. There are a couple of guys who are always taking my mother to the places that my father doesn't want to go."

"That's a little different."

"Doesn't matter. It's too late for that now anyway. But we can still make the most of the situation. We'll double date."

"We'll—*what?*"

"Now that you've got the list pared down, I need to make a final decision. So I'll have to spend a little time with each of these women—"

"Might not be a bad idea," she muttered.

He decided to be charitable and ignore the sarcasm. "—without making it seem that I'm devoting myself to her and excluding all the others. So if we make it a foursome—you, me, your husband, and the woman of the moment—it will all be more casual, and—"

"And not very practical, I'm afraid." Macey took a deep breath. "Look, I'm only going to say this once, so pay attention for a change, all right? I used to be married."

"Used to be?" Derek said slowly.

"He died three years ago."

Derek felt as if she'd slugged him right under the breastbone.

Her voice was soft and low and sad. "The doctors said that Jack was far too young to have the kind of cancer that killed him. That's why they didn't find it in time. I'm sorry if that interferes with your plans, Derek—but you're on your own now. Good night."

He was still reeling when she very gently closed the door behind her.

*   *   *

The flowers arrived at the office only a few minutes after Macey did. Ellen signed for them and carried the vase into Macey's office.

The arrangement was so huge that the combination of the vase and Ellen looked like a flowering shrub which had grown legs. Macey stared in astonishment as Ellen maneuvered the flowers through the doorway.

Roses, lilies, daisies, carnations—it looked as if someone had jammed the entire contents of a sizable floral shop into a five-gallon bucket without regard to color, style, or shape. The stems stuck out every which way. Though Ellen set the vase on the far corner of the desk, a branch of something white stretched out so far it was almost tickling Macey's nose, while on the opposite side of the arrangement, a stem of lilies actually brushed the office wall.

She was blocked in behind her desk by a bouquet.

"There's a card here somewhere," Ellen said breathlessly. "I got a glimpse of it when the delivery man set the vase down. But it's sort of like hunting buried treasure now."

Macey finally found the envelope hiding under a droopy yellow mum. Inside was a plain white card on which had been sketched a small black animal with a raised tail and a white stripe down its back, and the words, *So I'm a skunk. I admit it. I hope the flowers will smell better to you than I do.* It was not signed.

She leaned back in her chair and laughed till she had to wipe tears from her eyes. Hardly the reaction Derek would have hoped for, she supposed, but it seemed pretty much par for the course to her.

Robert came out of his office to see what all the noise was about. Macey slid the card smoothly into the pocket of her suit jacket and said, nodding toward the vase, "A thank-you from Derek McConnell."

His eyes brightened. "You got the problem solved, then?"

Beats me, but I guess we'll find out sooner or later.

But that was hardly an answer that Robert would find acceptable, so Macey opted to dodge the question. "I did everything I could."

"Fantastic. I must start watching the papers for an announcement."

Macey tried to hide her smile. "That'll be a new experience for you, Robert—reading the society pages for engagements."

"Society? I meant the business pages—looking for when he's named CEO."

Oh. I'd almost forgotten that part. "Of course."

Robert rubbed his hands together. "This is going to be terrific, Macey. If he says thank-you with temp jobs on the same scale he does with flowers, we'll need two new offices."

He was gone before Macey could suggest that it might not be smart to go looking for real estate just yet.

As for Macey herself, she decided that she wouldn't be reading the business pages—or the society section, either. Though in fact, whenever it happened, she would hardly be able to escape the news. Now that Clara was back in touch with the world, reading the newspapers and talking to her friend Enid, she would certainly hear about the announcement. And just as certainly, she'd tell Macey. Clara might even go to the wedding, and if she was invited to bring a companion she'd no doubt ask Macey to accompany her.

And I suppose as the matchmaker, you'll to be asked

to give a toast, she mocked herself. *Knock it off, Phillips. It's not your business anymore.*

She pulled the card with the little skunk on it out of her pocket and put it safely under the pen tray in her desk drawer. "Ellen? Go find some more containers and we'll try out your flower-arranging skills."

She was still with Ellen several hours later, going over the results of the woman's performance review and role-playing her first job assignment, when the receptionist tapped on Macey's door.

"Lunchtime," Louise said briskly.

Macey felt a trickle of exasperation. Louise knew better than to interrupt when she was in a training session. Besides, Macey had never before thought her receptionist was a clock-watcher. What had gotten into her? "I know what time it is, Louise. Just give me a couple of minutes to finish with Ellen, and then I'll cover up front while you go to lunch."

"No, I mean it's *your* lunchtime. Ellen can cover for me—she's been doing it for a couple of days anyway, while you've been gone."

"Fine," Macey said levelly. "Thank you very much for the reminder, Louise, but I'll go when I'm ready." *I'm not hungry, anyway.*

Ellen took one look over Louise's shoulder and muttered, "If you're not ready this minute, Macey, you're crazy."

Macey maneuvered past the vase on the corner of her desk and went to see what was going on.

Derek was leaning against the end of Louise's desk, his ankles crossed, facing Macey's office door. Draped over his shoulder was a blanket, and in one arm he held a brown paper bag that was stuffed to the bursting point and had a loaf of French bread protruding from the top.

"Thanks for the flowers," she said. "Of course now my office smells like a toxic spill at the perfume factory, but I appreciate the sentiment."

"That's why I thought we'd have lunch at the park instead."

"Self-defense?"

"In the open air, you might be able to stand being around the aroma of skunk."

He sounded serious, but she didn't miss the smile lurking in his eyes. And to think she'd once wondered whether he possessed any charm at all…. "I'll get my jacket."

She waited till they were out of the office, and then she said, without looking at him, "It's okay, Derek. Really. It was a natural mistake. You don't have to go to such trouble to make it up to me."

"I don't?" He stopped abruptly in the middle of the sidewalk. "Well, in that case, lunch is off. Back to work with you."

Macey kept right on walking. "On the other hand, I'm sure you'll feel a thousand percent better once you've made amends, so who am I to deny you the opportunity to abase yourself? What's for lunch?"

The park was just a block from Peterson Temps. It wasn't much of a park, actually, just a tiny green space intended to break the monotony of the storefronts, with a few benches and a couple of flower beds that were beginning to look bedraggled with autumn coming on.

Derek had obviously scoped the place out ahead of time, for he didn't hesitate at the edge of the park but led her across to the far corner, where a row of honeysuckle bushes, heavy with red fruit, protected a patch of sunlit grass. The breeze rustled through the leaves, but the dense bushes broke its force and kept it from chilling them. High above in an oak tree a cardinal sang.

Macey helped spread out the blanket and sank down on a corner of it. "Nice," she said. "Solar heat, live background music, even a nice log to serve as a backrest."

"And a simple picnic lunch." Derek began to unpack the bag.

In one sense, Macey concluded, it was a very simple lunch. He'd brought bread and butter, cheese, olives, and fruit. But the bread was so fresh it was still warm; the butter was rich, and there were four varieties of cheese and two of olives. She hadn't seen so many kinds of fruit lined up anywhere but a supermarket. And from the bottom of the bag he pulled out a thermal mug full of the best cappuccino she'd ever tasted.

He had, however, forgotten to bring anything to slice the bread with. So they tore chunks off the loaf, and he reduced the cheese and fruit to irregular slices with his Swiss army knife.

The tiny blade slipped as he cut up an apple, and Derek swore. "I knew I should have sharpened this thing after I used it to cut duct tape the other day."

"Doesn't it have more than one blade?"

"Yes, but I broke the tip off the other one when I used it to pry the lid off a paint can."

"Well, be careful," Macey warned. "You don't want to slice a finger so badly you can't draw anymore."

"Did you like the little skunk? That's just a sketch— it's more cartooning than art. But it comes in handy sometimes when we're designing packaging, labels, stuff like that. It's easier to draw an idea than to put it into words."

"Maybe it's easier for you." She reached for a bunch of grapes. "Not for everybody."

"I've always drawn a little. Just like I've always known

I wanted to run my father's company." He folded up the knife. "What got you into the temp business?"

She hesitated.

"You don't have to tell me, if you don't want."

"No, it's all right. It was after Jack died. I had to take some time off work, and the bills were pretty steep."

"No life insurance?" His voice was gentle.

"We never got around to buying any. When you're twenty-five, you don't think you need it, and there are a lot of other things you want more. I went back to work as soon as I could, of course, and I moved in with Jack's aunt to cut expenses. But my regular paycheck still wasn't enough to make a dent in the debts, so I started to take some temp jobs for a little extra income."

"And you liked the work?"

Macey nodded. "I liked the constant change, and the pay was good. By the time Robert offered to make me office manager, I'd finally gotten my head above water, and I gave up my other job so I could be at home with Clara more."

"Her idea, or yours? You staying home, I mean."

"A little of both. She took it pretty hard when Jack died." Macey leaned back against the log, savoring her cappuccino. "Thanks for lunch. You can apologize to me anytime you want."

Derek ate the last crumb of cheddar. "I'm not exactly apologizing," he admitted. "At least not entirely. I thought maybe I could take you up on your offer from last night."

To discuss the six women she'd left on the list. Macey knew she should have expected something of the sort, once he'd had a chance to consider the names she'd handed him.

And it was probably just as well, she thought, for her

to be reminded that he'd only gone to all the trouble of arranging a picnic in the park because he couldn't take her somewhere like Arcadia—at least, not without raising every eyebrow in St. Louis so high that baldness wouldn't be a problem anymore.

"Finally got around to looking at the list, did you?" She tried to keep her voice light.

"Yeah. Why those six, and not some of the others?"

She slid down a little and turned so she was at more of an angle to him, rather than sitting side by side against the log. "I wondered if that would happen." She was talking more to herself than to him.

"If what would happen?"

"Whether you'd be surprised when you looked at the list. If you might be startled—maybe even disappointed—because one particular name wasn't on it."

"I still don't understand what you mean."

Macey pulled her knees up and wrapped her arms around them. "Have you ever had so much trouble making up your mind between two options that you ended up flipping a coin?"

"Sure. Everybody has."

"But then did you go along with what the coin toss told you? Or did you find yourself wanting to flip it again—maybe go two out of three? Because either way, whether you were satisfied with the coin's advice or not, after you made that flip you knew what you really wanted to do. Tossing a coin just cuts through all the intellectual stuff and tells you how you really feel deep down inside."

"So what does flipping a quarter have to do with this?" He reached into his shirt pocket and dangled the list under her nose.

"Because if there's one name that you really want to ask me about, Derek, and you feel a need to know why it's not there, then that's the woman you ought to marry—not one of the six on the list.''

Derek frowned. ''So you're telling me this piece of paper is nothing more than a psychological trick you made up.''

She was annoyed. ''No, it's not. At least, I didn't set it up that way—and if I had, I sure wouldn't tell you about it. But if that's how it works, at least you'll know what you want. *Who* you want.''

The silence grew. Macey took another sip of her cappuccino. All of a sudden, it wasn't so good anymore. The brew had gone cold, and it tasted almost bitter.

''Well?'' she said finally. ''Who is she, Derek?''

He shook his head. ''I wasn't thinking about anybody in particular.''

Macey wasn't sure whether to believe him or not. He sounded sincere, but if he was telling the truth, why had it taken him so long to answer?

He laid the paper down on the blanket between them and tapped a finger squarely in the middle of the list of names. ''I just wondered what was so special about these six. What made them stand out to you?''

''You want to know what I saw so you can look for the same qualities to admire? I'm honored by the faith you're putting in me, Derek, but I'm not the one who's going to have to live with this woman. Don't you think it's time *you*—''

''I just want to know what you based this list on.''

''All right,'' she said slowly. ''I guess it's fair to ask what standards I measured by. But you see, the deciding factor was actually more what *wasn't* special about these six.''

''Now you've really lost me, Macey.''

She sighed. ''The others—the ones I took off the list—

all stood out from the crowd, all right, but for reasons that were less than pleasant.''

"For instance?''

"One of them nearly knocked Clara over at the door of Arcadia.''

"Accidents—''

"—happen, yes. And I'm not saying it wasn't accidental. But she could have stopped to make sure Clara was all right—it wasn't like she was rushing inside to stop somebody from hemorrhaging. She didn't bother.''

"Which one of them did that?''

Macey gave him the name.

Derek's eyebrows shot up. "I have never seen her being anything but perfectly polite.''

"Of course you haven't,'' Macey said. She was beginning to feel a little cross. "And you won't until after you've married someone else and she's convinced you're completely out of range. Or until you've married *her,* and she feels she doesn't have to put on a show anymore.'' She set her cup down. "I really have to get back to work—and you probably do too. I'll help gather up the mess.''

"Don't bother. I'll get it.''

"Are you sure?''

He smiled. "It's my favorite kind of kitchen cleanup—everything goes in the garbage can except the blanket.'' He stood up and offered a hand to pull Macey to her feet.

"Thanks again.'' It felt awkward just to turn around and walk away. "Derek—let me know how it goes.''

"Sure,'' he said.

She forced herself to smile. "If it all works out, will you write me a recommendation? I just might be looking for a job someday—and maybe there's a future in matchmaking.''

He laughed.

Macey walked back toward Peterson Temps with her head bowed. The breeze had sharpened, and outside the sheltered little corner of the park it felt positively cold.

Would he actually keep her informed?

And—the even bigger question—did she really, truly want him to?

CHAPTER SIX

WHEN Macey came into the town house carrying two bags of groceries, Clara was sitting at the small kitchen table contemplating a bare, plain white china plate which sat in front of her.

"Have you started dieting?" Macey asked lightly. "Because if you have, you'll simply have to give it up right now. I just picked up everything we need for beef stroganoff."

Clara didn't look up. "It'll keep till tomorrow."

Macey stopped in the middle of the room and stared at Clara. "You love beef stroganoff as much as I do. Why would you want to put it off?"

Clara shrugged. "I'm guessing that you might. Don't start cooking till you've returned your phone calls."

Macey tried to set the bags down carefully. "Okay—explain. Who called?"

"A man. Fairly young by the sound of his voice. He left a number." Clara picked up a ruler and a felt-tipped marker and began to make small dots at regular intervals around the rim of the plate.

Macey picked up a slip of paper from beside the phone. "No name?"

"Don't blame me. I asked, but he seemed to want to be the mystery man."

Derek. Macey's heart beat just a little faster. No doubt he would rather have seemed rude than to tell Clara who he was—it would invite too many questions about why her old friend Enid's son was calling Clara's niece.

The number didn't look familiar, but then it wouldn't—Macey hadn't ever called him at home. Hadn't been able to, in fact, because his number wasn't in the phone book. That was one of the reasons she'd actually gone over to his loft that night to deliver the list, taking the pizza that she'd ended up sharing with Ted because Derek hadn't been at home.

Two days had passed since their picnic in the park, and she hadn't heard a word from him. Had he called to tell her he'd made his selection? If so, no wonder he hadn't left a message with Clara. *"Tell her Derek McConnell called and I've decided to marry Rebecca."* Or Emily. Or Constance...

No—a message like that would stir up way too much curiosity.

But it hardly seemed possible that he'd decided already, anyway. In the span of just over forty-eight hours—and spread across a couple of workdays, at that—how could he have possibly fit in enough time with six different women to choose one of them over the others? Because somehow Macey didn't think he would have settled for the first one on the list without taking a closer look at the rest, even if that woman had managed to impress him. Just because Macey had the sneaking suspicion that all of them were pretty much interchangeable didn't mean that Derek saw them in the same light.

In fact, she thought, in a weird sort of way the man was actually kind of a romantic...

Stop dithering around about it and ask him, Macey. Call him back.

She dialed the phone and held it against her ear with one shoulder while she unpacked the groceries.

A male voice answered. But it wasn't Derek's voice.

Macey frowned. Surely no one else would answer

Derek's phone in that casual way—and why would anyone but Derek be answering it at all?

They wouldn't. Which must mean her guess was wrong, and it hadn't been Derek who had left that message in the first place. She told herself it was ridiculous to be disappointed, but it didn't help much.

"Hello?" the voice said again.

Long training kicked in. "This is Macey Phillips. I had a message to call this number."

"Macey! I was afraid you weren't going to call me back."

She still didn't recognize the voice. "Excuse me, but do I know you?"

"Oh, that's right—I always forget that people sound so much different in person. It's Ira."

Ira. Macey rummaged through her brain. Was he a business acquaintance? Surely not, because he'd called her at home, and that was something she would never have encouraged a client to do.

It must be personal, then. And it was obviously someone she'd actually met, not just spoken to on the phone. But who—?

"Ira Branson," he said, sounding just a little impatient. "From the symphony party. Derek McConnell's friend."

Well, at least he got my name right this time.

"Look, I don't blame you for being peeved at me for taking so long to call."

He thought she was only pretending not to remember him? Macey wondered if he actually thought she'd been sitting by the phone day after day, waiting for it to ring. "Heavens, no. I've been so busy I hadn't given it a thought."

He laughed as if that was the funniest story he'd ever heard. "I wanted to call you right away, but I couldn't.

I've been trying for days now to get your phone number. You forgot to give it to me at the party.''

No, Ira, that's not the kind of thing I forget. If I'd wanted you to have the number...

''Do you have any idea how many women named Marcie Phillips live in St. Louis?''

So much for giving him credit. ''It's Macey,'' she said. Of course, she told herself wryly, she was hardly in a position to complain no matter what he called her, since she hadn't remembered him—or his name—at all.

''Yeah, I finally figured that out. Anyway, I wondered if you'd like to go out with me.''

''It's very kind of you, Ira, but I'm afraid I can't.''

''Wait, I haven't even told you yet what the invitation is.''

Noticed that, did you? Very perceptive.

''There's a party tonight and I thought you'd like to go with me. It's another fund-raiser, but this one's for the zoo. You know, cute fuzzy animals all over the place, that sort of thing. I know women love that kind of thing.'' He paused. ''Look, you're not angry with me for asking so late, are you? I know it's not much notice, but I just got your number today.''

''I'm sorry, Ira, but I've already made plans for this evening.'' *Put together a beef stroganoff, check all my silk flower arrangements to be certain they're not getting root-bound, rearrange the words in the dictionary from shortest to longest instead of alphabetically...*

''What about tomorrow night? There's a Halloween thing I thought you might like.''

''I have plans.'' She put a skillet on the range and reached for the olive oil. Couldn't the man take a hint?

Clara looked up from the china plate. ''You don't have to stay home for my sake.''

Macey shook her head, hoping Clara would get the message. She didn't think Ira would have been able to overhear her since Clara was all the way across the kitchen, but the last thing she needed was for him to feel encouraged.

"Sunday?" Ira asked.

She was actually starting to feel sorry for him. *Careful, Macey—that's dangerous.* "Ira, it's very kind of you, but I'm not dating at all right now."

He made a sound that resembled a snort. "If you're sitting at home waiting for McConnell, you might as well get over it."

"My plans have nothing to do with…" Macey turned to reach for a spatula, noticed that Clara was watching her, and swallowed the name just in time. "I think you've misunderstood the situation, Ira."

"What else am I supposed to think?"

You might consider the idea that I'm simply not attracted to you.

"Anyway, if you're trying to give him the silent treatment by staying home," Ira went on, "you should know it's not working. I've seen him several times lately, and never twice with the same woman. Pretty soon people will be taking bets about who he'll turn up with next."

"That's very interesting. Not that it has anything to do with me, but—"

"I'm just telling you, there's no point in moping around waiting for him to come back to you. You might as well get out there and play the field yourself."

"I'll certainly keep that advice in mind," Macey said dryly.

"Good. Now how about Sunday? You didn't give me a chance to really ask you. There's a nice brunch at my country club."

Play the
Lucky
Hearts *Game*

and get...
2 FREE BOOKS
and a FREE MYSTERY GIFT...
yes! YOURS to KEEP!

I have scratched off the silver card. Please send me my *2 FREE BOOKS* and *FREE mystery GIFT*. I understand that I am under no obligation to purchase any books as explained on the back of this card.

Scratch Here!
then look below to see what your cards get you... 2 Free Books & a Free Mystery Gift!

386 HDL DU6V   186 HDL DU7D

FIRST NAME   LAST NAME

ADDRESS

APT.#   CITY

STATE/PROV.   ZIP/POSTAL CODE   (H-RA-08/03)

Twenty-one gets you
2 FREE BOOKS
and a **FREE MYSTERY GIFT!**

Twenty gets you
2 FREE BOOKS!

Nineteen gets you
1 FREE BOOK!

TRY AGAIN!

Offer limited to one per household and not valid to current Harlequin Romance® subscribers. All orders subject to approval.

The Harlequin Reader Service® — Here's how it works:

"I've already—"

"You've made plans for the entire weekend—I get it. A lady never accepts the first invitation. Well, you think it over. I might check back with you in a day or two, though you shouldn't count on it."

I'll be holding my breath in anxious anticipation. "Good night, Ira."

She put the phone down and dumped beef chunks into the skillet. The angry sizzle of the hot oil mimicked her mood.

Though she supposed Ira had meant well. At least, she'd try to give him the benefit of the doubt. Surely nobody could be that annoying on purpose.

Clara held up the plate at arm's length, inspecting it. "You shouldn't turn down a date to stay home on my account, Macey."

"I didn't."

"But you did turn him down, and pretty definitely. Saying you weren't dating at all is about the firmest excuse I've ever heard."

"It's not an excuse. It's the truth, Clara." Macey stirred the beef. "I'm just not interested in dating."

"Nobody's saying you have to get married. But what's the problem with you going out with a man now and then? Just having some fun? Who would that hurt?"

"People like Ira," Macey said. "All I did was go to a fund-raiser. It wasn't even really a party, and it certainly wasn't a date. Now he's got the idea that I'm available, and worse yet, that I'm interested in him and only pretending to be coy."

"Ira? Is that the man you've been working for?"

"No. Why?"

"That's too bad. I thought maybe that was going to turn into something. You were going somewhere with him pretty regularly for a while, and then *pffft*. It turns to dust.''

"Well, that's the nature of my business, Clara. Temporary.''

"Don't get tart with me, young lady.''

"I'm sorry. But I wasn't dating him, so please don't get confused.'' Macey looked over the older woman's shoulder. "What are you doing to that poor plate?''

"Trying to decide how to paint it. I started my porcelain-painting class this morning, and this is my first project.''

Macey eyed the cryptic squiggles and dots which almost covered the plate. "It's...very modern.''

"That's just the guide marks so I'll get the design on straight. I'm going to paint a wreath of violets on this one.''

"Sounds pretty.''

"After I do a few practice pieces to learn the techniques and get my hands steady, maybe I'll make you a whole set of china.'' Clara's voice took on a wistful note. "I've always felt bad about you having to sell your wedding dishes after Jack died.''

"I needed the money at the time. And though I'd love to have you make me something, I really don't need china. I'll probably never entertain in that style.''

"You never know what you might need,'' Clara said vaguely. "Do you really like the idea of violets? Or would you rather have a different flower? Or just a pattern? Because I should practice painting what you want.''

"You should paint whatever you like, Clara. If it ends up being an entire set, that's lovely, but I'd think it would be very dull to paint the same thing over and over till you had a service for twelve.''

The phone rang and Macey picked it up. She half expected it was Ira calling back, now that he'd given her a few minutes to regret the magnificent opportunity she'd turned down.

But this time the caller was Derek. "Macey? I was hoping it would be you who answered."

She tried to fight off the sudden breathless feeling that had hit her at the sound of his voice. "I'll bet you were," she said, shooting a sideways look at Clara—who was obviously listening. "I hear via the grapevine that you've been busy."

"Has my mother been talking to your aunt again?"

"No—another source entirely." Macey stirred the cubes of meat so they'd brown more evenly. "How are things going?"

"These are actually the best six names you could come up with? You didn't accidentally give me the list of rejects instead?"

"No, that's the only list. You've already run through all of them?"

"In two days? I'm not Casanova, Macey."

All appearances to the contrary. "Then why are you giving up already?"

"I didn't say I was giving up. In fact I have another date tonight, and—damn, I'm running late. I just wanted you to know that so far I'm not excited by your choices."

"Then it's probably just as well I haven't sent you a bill for my time yet," Macey said gently. "Now run along and get dressed up so you'll make the best possible impression on the lady of the evening."

He was swearing—and she was smiling—when Macey put the phone down.

On Saturday morning Derek left a message on the answering machine while Macey and Clara were having breakfast at the neighborhood café. "I'm looking for you, Macey," was all he said. He left no name and no number.

Clara looked a little concerned. "He sounds like a nut-case."

"It's not some sort of threat," Macey said, and frowned. "At least, I don't think it is."

The phone rang just a couple of minutes later. When Macey answered, Derek said, "Come for a ride with me."

"I'm busy." She noticed a picture frame which had gotten knocked askew on the wall above the phone. The light reflecting from the front window turned the glass almost mirror-like, but when she reached up to shift it back into place the light changed and the picture inside, a snapshot of Jack at a barbecue, reappeared.

"You can't be busy yet," Derek argued. "You just got home."

"How would you know that? Have you been calling all morning to check?"

"No—I've been keeping an eye on your front door for the last hour. I'm parked across the street."

Macey checked her watch. "You've been out there for an hour already? The only conclusion I can draw is that it must have been a very long date last night and you're just on your way home now. Otherwise you wouldn't be out running around so early. Oh, I know what that means! We struck pay dirt last night, so you decided to swing by here on your way home just to thank me. That's such a sweet thought, Derek. Who's the lucky woman going to be?"

"You wish. Are you coming out or shall I come in and get you?"

"Oh, by all means come in," Macey said sweetly. "You can meet Clara. She's very curious about you." And a good thing it was, she thought, that Clara had gone up to her room and wasn't within hearing distance at the moment. "Just think, the two of you can drink coffee and talk about all of your mutual acquaintances."

He muttered something under his breath.

Macey smiled. "Does that mean you've changed your mind about coming in?" She didn't wait for an answer, because she was honestly curious. "The date was really that bad? Which one was this?"

"Rebecca."

"Really? I thought she was a serious contender."

"So far you're zero for three, Macey. If this were a baseball game, you'd have been called out on strikes."

"Unfortunately, I was never very good at baseball. Wait a minute—did you say you've eliminated *three?* When have you had time?"

"It didn't take much time to throw Constance off the list. I ran into her last night, and by the time she'd giggled her way through a five-minute conversation I was ready to commit murder."

"In that case, it was probably a good idea not to actually marry her," Macey said solemnly. "But maybe she was just nervous. Are you quite certain you're approaching these women properly? I mean, take last night for an example. If you were actually supposed to be out with Rebecca but in fact you were carrying on with Constance—"

"*Carrying on?* That can't really be what you just said. My battery must be going dead. Hold on, I'm coming in."

The phone went silent in her hand. Macey swore, punched the off button, and called up the stairs, "Clara! I'll be back in a little while!" She opened the front door just as Derek was raising his hand to the bell.

He had definitely been home since his date last night—

or else it had been a very casual date, because he was wearing jeans and a leather jacket.

He looked from her face to the windbreaker she was carrying over her arm, and raised his eyebrows.

"I changed my mind," she said. "Some fresh air sounds like a great idea." She slid her hand around his elbow and tried to urge him off the front steps.

Derek didn't budge. "I wonder why you don't want me to meet Clara."

"Because the first thing she'll do is tell your mother and then you'll really be in the chicken soup. Isn't that reason enough?"

"It should be—but somehow I don't think it's *my* welfare you're concerned about. Now what were you saying about my approach?" He led her down the sidewalk to a candy-apple-red convertible and opened the passenger door.

Macey stopped short, eying the folded-down top. "I don't think I'm up for this much fresh air."

"It blows the cobwebs out of your brain."

Macey didn't doubt it. The little car looked as if it was capable of mach speed, and considering the mood he was in... "Can I drive?"

"Over my dead body."

"Then I'm not going for a ride. I have more important things to do today, anyway." She leaned against the car. "That attitude of yours is exactly the kind of thing I'm talking about. *Over my dead body,*" she mimicked. "I suspect you're coming on too strong. Being too intense."

"Being focused is a good thing."

"Perhaps it is—but the word I was thinking of wasn't *focused.* It was *inflexible.*"

He closed the door and braced a hand on the top of the windshield, tapping his fingertips against the glass. "I have to give you credit, Macey. It takes a lot of nerve to critique my methods when you're not even there to see what's going on.''

"Well, that much is only common sense, Derek. It's tough enough to get through a first date when it's just dinner. When the stakes include a whole lifetime—''

"You surely don't think I'm fool enough to tell these women what I'm contemplating."

"Heavens, no," Macey said airily. "Why would you give your prospective bride any say in the matter? There will be plenty of time to let the one you choose know what you're thinking after you've made up your mind. Because how could she possibly be anything but thrilled to win the honor of playing your wife—even if she didn't know ahead of time that she was auditioning for the role?''

His eyes narrowed. "Don't let concern for my feelings keep you from expressing your opinions clearly, Macey." His voice was dry.

"Thanks, I won't. But even if they didn't have the details, they were probably feeling the pressure anyway, just because you're under so much stress. Give everybody a break, Derek.''

"I don't have time. Besides, you seem to have misunderstood what's going on here. I'm not exactly taking these women out on dates, so the pressure on them isn't nearly as intense as you seem to think."

"What do you mean, you're not taking them out on dates?''

"I can't," he said bluntly. "Having already informed the chairman of the board that I'm engaged, I can hardly be seen having an intimate supper with Rita and then dancing the night away with Lou.''

That was a problem. "If you went to a movie," Macey mused, "you could at least hold hands in the dark."

"And exactly what would going to a movie tell me about a woman, beyond whether or not she likes butter on her popcorn?"

"You've got a good point there," Macey conceded. "Especially because I can already tell you that they don't—none of them. Butter has far too many calories. So if dates are out, what are you doing?"

"Trying to check them out in situations that are public enough not to leave the wrong impression—with them or with anyone else."

"I don't think you're succeeding," she said frankly. "At least, Ira told me that people were going to start betting on who you'd be seeing next."

"Ira Branson?" He folded his arms across his chest and looked her over. "When did you talk to him?"

"Yesterday. He invited me to some fund-raiser last night."

"The one for the zoo? You turned him down? Macey, that would have been perfect. You could have been right there to lend me a hand, and nobody would even have wondered why, as long as you were with Ira."

"Don't you think that would be a shabby way to treat Ira?" Macey held up both hands, palms out. "I take it back. Don't even try to answer that. What am I thinking? A man who carries on a serious courtship at a fund-raiser for the zoo, without letting the women he's courting know what he's got in mind, couldn't possibly understand the finer points of dating etiquette. Anyway, now that I've answered your question, I'll be going back inside."

"What's so important today that you can't come for a ride?"

"Lots of things," Macey said crisply. "I didn't sign

on to work around the clock. What's so important about the ride?''

''I was hoping you'd do me a favor. I broke one of my mother's glasses, but when I called the store to have them send her a replacement, they said the company doesn't make that exact thing anymore.''

''And you don't know what to give her instead—but you think I'm supposed to? Are you listening to yourself, Derek?''

He shrugged. ''Women think differently about these things.''

''You can say that again.'' If he hadn't looked at her like a three-year-old who had just been scolded, she might have walked away. Instead she sighed. ''I can give you an hour, tops. Agreed?''

''You got it.'' Almost ostentatiously, he looked at his wristwatch, then helped her into the car and walked around to slide behind the wheel. The engine roared to life and the convertible shot into the street at a speed that pressed Macey deep into the leather seat.

''Can you take it a little easier?'' she asked breathlessly. ''If I had a hat, it would be three blocks behind us by now—and I feel like my hair's about to follow.''

The traffic light changed ahead of them and Derek shifted gears and roared through the intersection. ''I'm not the one who's in a hurry,'' he pointed out. ''Besides, we're not going as fast as it seems. It only feels that way because of the wind and the way the car's engineered to sit so close to the street.''

''Thanks for the physics lesson, but I'd just as soon not have a tooth jarred out if you hit a speed bump unexpectedly.''

He looked injured. ''Jarred? In this car?'' But he slowed down.

Fast or not, he was an excellent driver, and once she got used to the sensation of the wind whipping her hair, Macey enjoyed the drive. He was right about the cobwebs, she thought. The fresh air was definitely clearing out her brain. She practically didn't have a sensible thought left to her name.

That phenomenon might have explained why she actually asked him how he planned to check out the last three remaining names on the list—because, she told herself as soon as the question was out, it was dead sure that she didn't really want to know.

"There's a Halloween party tonight, so with any luck I should be able to catch at least two of them there." He shot a sideways look at her. "Did Ira invite you to the Halloween party?"

"If it's the same party, yes. And no, I'm not going to call him back and beg him to renew the invitation so I can come and help you out. At a costume party, you don't need help anyway—nobody will know who you are, so you can circulate freely."

"I'd rather go to a movie," he grumbled. "Alone."

"Brace up, it's almost over. Three down, three to go. And you know what they say, Derek—the item you're searching for is always in the last place you check."

"That's because when you find it, you quit looking."

"Of course. But the saying's still true."

"So are you suggesting I just cancel Liz and Rita and skip straight to Emily?"

"Oh, no—because then Emily *wouldn't* be last, and you'd have to go looking for Liz and Rita again."

"You're a whole lot of help," he grumbled.

Macey gave him her most tranquil smile. "All I can do is try."

*   *   *

She was trying all right, Derek thought. Trying his patience.

At least on Saturday downtown traffic wasn't as heavy, though parking outside the main branch of the city's largest department store was atrocious. Half the city seemed to have gone shopping this morning.

He noticed Macey eyeing him with interest while he maneuvered the convertible into the last available spot within blocks.

"I thought we'd be going to one of the mall stores," she said.

"But this one has the best inventory."

"As a matter of fact, it does. I'm just surprised you know that."

"Rebecca told me," he admitted. "So I guess I'd have to say last night was only ninety-five percent wasted instead of being a complete loss."

"I'm glad you got something out of it," Macey murmured. "At least this store used to be the best. I haven't been inside in years. I don't suppose it was just a basic water goblet you broke."

"I'm afraid not." Derek held the main door for her and wondered if it would be prying to ask why she hadn't been shopping for so long. Though that wasn't exactly what she'd said, he reminded himself.

Macey stopped a clerk to ask for directions and led the way to the elevator.

When they stepped off on the housewares floor, he almost collided with a lighted display case full of glass pieces that looked as if they had been left out in the cold until frost formed over the designs. "These are pretty," he said.

"They're gorgeous," Macey said. "I've always adored Lalique."

"Maybe I could get her a nice vase."

"You certainly could. How much is that one?"

He bent to look at the price tag and choked.

She turned around, eyebrows raised, to inspect him. "What's the matter, Derek? You sound as if you've been hit with an ax."

"There's a comma in that price."

"Yes, my friend," Macey said. "Isn't your mother worth it?"

He looked at her sharply. She looked innocent, but there had been a malicious note in her voice. "I dropped a glass, Macey—I didn't systematically shatter every single one she owns."

"So the answer is no?" Macey relented. "Fortunately for you, she wouldn't want a vase, anyway. She's got a thousand of them already."

Suspicion chewed at him. "And exactly how would you know that?"

"You can trust me on this, Derek. Vases, like coat hangers, multiply when left in dark cupboards—particularly when the cupboard belongs to a woman like your mother." She paused beside a long polished dining table. It was fully set, complete down to the last napkin, wineglass, and knife rest, but each place displayed a different kind of china. "Now that's an idea. Why not an assortment of patterns?"

"Are you talking to me?"

"No, to myself. Clara's threatening to paint a set of china for me. I was just wondering what it would look like if she did each piece with a different flower."

"Like a garden that's badly in need of weeding."

"You're probably right. What kind of a glass was it you broke?"

He looked around, feeling helpless. "Something like those over there, I guess."

But Macey wasn't listening. One of the china patterns, the one at the head of the table, had obviously caught her eye. "This is my china. The pattern I had when I was married." She picked up the dinner plate and turned it over to look more closely. "Ouch—it's even more expensive now. Clara's right—I should have held on to it."

"Why didn't you?"

"Between the hospital bills and the funeral costs, I needed the money." She set the plate down with a firm click and turned away. "Now, which glass was it?"

Derek stared at the plate. It was pure white, with a thin black rim, a red block in the center and a silver triangle off to one side.

Interesting, he thought. If she'd asked him to guess which pattern she liked best, that would have been the last one on the table that he'd have chosen.

On the other hand, he reminded himself, she was still turning up with ghastly new earrings just about every time he saw her, so what did he know about her taste?

He turned to follow Macey over to the cabinet he'd pointed out and came face-to-face with his mother.

"Hello, dear," Enid McConnell murmured. "And what might you be doing here on a nice day like this? Thinking about choosing a china pattern?"

CHAPTER SEVEN

WHAT playful trick of fate had inspired his mother to go shopping on this very day and in this very store? Because, much as Derek would have liked to blame someone, it couldn't be anything but fate.

Replacing a broken cocktail glass hadn't been the top item on his agenda when he'd left home this morning, though he'd had every intention of doing something about it sooner or later. But since he hadn't even known himself where he'd be, there was no point in looking for a hidden meaning in his mother's presence. Nobody could have tipped her off. It was sheer, stupid coincidence that she'd turned up.

It had to be, he told himself. Because the only other explanation was that his mother was learning to tune in on his thoughts like a radio receiver—and that would be a whole lot worse.

But of course she wasn't reading his mind, or she wouldn't have asked that particular question. *Thinking about choosing a china pattern?*

In fact, there was nothing further from his mind than china. But that didn't make the question any easier to answer, because the entire subject was a minefield. He opened his mouth, but the only sound that came out was halfway between a gulp and a hiccup.

Macey came up beside him.

Derek wished she'd had enough sense to keep her distance and pretend to be looking at something else. His mother might not have seen them together, but now there would be no doubt in her mind.

"He'll be all right in a minute, Mrs. McConnell," Macey patted his arm comfortingly and smiled at his mother. "To answer your question, though—no, we're not shopping for china."

Now why couldn't he have said that? Straightforward, calm, to the point. Macey really was a treasure. No wonder Robert thought so highly of his office manager.

Of course it was fairly easy to be composed and candid when dealing with someone else's mother. It was just like being frank and composed when talking to an employee.

Macey went on, "Actually, we're looking for the perfect crystal."

If the entire eight-story department store had fallen on his head, Derek couldn't have been more stunned. What was she going to do next? Formally invite his mother to the wedding?

So much for Robert's assurance that Macey Phillips wouldn't try to snag him for herself. Instead, this female shark had been circling for nearly a week, waiting for him to be off guard. Waiting for the moment when he'd be easy prey.

It was no particular comfort to realize that he'd handed her the opportunity. Asking her advice on a gift for his mother—what the hell had he been thinking?

Macey waved a hand in front of his nose. "Breathe, Derek," she ordered. "You're getting cross-eyed from lack of oxygen. Come on, you can do it." She held out a hand to Enid. "We met at Arcadia, if you remember."

"Of course. You were with your husband's Aunt Clara."

Derek managed a gasp of air. There was his salvation, he thought. It was his mother who had told him that

Macey was married. As long as Enid McConnell believed that, she couldn't possibly take the shopping-for-crystal story seriously. Now he just had to get Macey away from his mother before Enid figured out the truth...

"Please accept my sympathies, Macey," Enid said. "I didn't realize the day we met that you'd lost your husband."

Too late.

"Thank you," Macey said quietly. "I'm very glad to run into you, Mrs. McConnell."

I'll bet, Derek thought grimly. *It makes your scheme much easier to pull off.*

"Derek felt so badly about breaking your glass and not being able to find a replacement that he asked my advice on how to make it up to you." Macey made it sound as if it was no big deal after all.

Derek shot a look at his mother and noted that she looked neither surprised nor shocked. Maybe—just maybe—he'd misjudged Macey. Jumped to conclusions about what she was trying to accomplish.

Very carefully, he forced himself to relax. This up and down stuff was wearing him out in a hurry.

His mother was surveying him. "That's sweet of you, dear, but I know perfectly well it was an accident. It could have happened to anyone. The shock of the moment caused you to be distracted for an instant, that's all."

Macey frowned. "What was the shock of the moment?" she said under her breath.

Derek ignored her, and as he'd hoped, she gave it up.

"I thought," Macey went on, "that we'd be able to find a pattern which would at least be compatible with yours. Foolish of me to think that Derek could remember it well enough to compare. So this is even better—you can make a choice yourself."

"That's lovely of you, Derek, to let me choose a replacement." Enid McConnell looked around. "Let's see—what might I like?"

"Derek was admiring the case of Lalique," Macey murmured. "He thought perhaps the vase."

There was a note of mischief in her voice that made him want to smack her.

"But somehow I didn't think that would be quite right for you," she went on.

The expression on his mother's face was unreadable, but Derek could guess what it meant. Whether Enid McConnell wanted that vase or not, she wouldn't allow a snip of a young woman—one she didn't even know—to interpret and dictate her tastes.

The net result was that any minute now, because Macey had let herself run off at the mouth like that, he was going to be paying for a vase. And paying. And paying.

"At any rate, since you're here, Mrs. McConnell, you and Derek can make a choice and perhaps you'll excuse me."

Macey patted his arm again—just about the same way she'd say goodbye to a dog, Derek thought—and stepped away.

"Oh, no, dear." Enid McConnell linked her arm into Macey's. "You're quite right about the vase, by the way. How did you know I prefer clear glass to the decorated sort?"

In the midst of his own surprise, he derived a tiny bit of satisfaction from the fact that Macey seemed taken aback. And a little more, he admitted, because he wasn't going to find that vase on his credit card statement next month after all.

"I'd love to have your opinion," Enid went on, "because what I really came for today was to choose a new pattern. The glass Derek broke was older than he is, and so much of my wedding crystal is gone now that it's time for an entirely new set. It's just that I'm not sure what I want.''

The two of them moved off toward a lighted case lined with goblets and wineglasses. Macey cast a desperate-looking glance over her shoulder at him. Derek pretended to ignore it. She'd dug herself into this mess; let her work her own way out.

''Styles have changed so much,'' Enid McConnell went on, ''since I chose my patterns. And of course my tastes have changed as well, so I'm—''

Derek leaned one hip against a railing to make himself comfortable for what he could see might be a very long wait. Then, abruptly, he realized that letting the two of them get out of earshot was a very dumb move. He wasn't sure which one of them he distrusted more—though it didn't make much difference; either of them was clearly capable of causing trouble.

And not that he could actually do much in the way of damage control, either, because his tongue still felt as useless as if it were made of recycled chewing gum. But at least if he knew what they were discussing, he'd have a shot at defending himself.

He almost bumped into Macey as he came around the corner of a rack that held nothing but glass lamps and clocks.

His mother was pointing at a wineglass and saying something about the softly rounded lines, but she paused in midsentence and looked thoughtfully at him. ''Derek, I'm sure you're bored silly by all this. Don't let us keep you from the other important things you must need to do.''

''I hadn't planned anything else for this morning.''

Enid pursed her lips. "You're only going to make this take longer, you realize, if you can't bear to be away from Macey's side."

Now there's a scary thought. However, Derek realized, she'd given him the excuse he needed. He almost snapped his fingers in relief. "Macey, you told me you only had an hour to spare this morning, and that's more than up. I'll take you home—"

"I'll be happy to take her home," Enid said. "I can choose crystal anytime, and I'd like to see Clara again, anyway."

"Why don't the two of you stay here and look," Macey murmured, "and I'll take a cab."

If she thought she was going to abandon him and run away, she could think again. Derek took her firmly by the arm. "See you later, Mom."

Macey resisted for an instant and then gave in with a smile and a shrug of the shoulders—no doubt both intended for Enid's benefit.

Back on the street, in the relative safety and anonymity of the crowd, Derek stopped in the middle of the sidewalk and scowled at her. *"We're looking for the perfect crystal,"* he mimicked. "Were you *trying* to cause trouble?"

"I certainly didn't give her any ideas that weren't already in her mind," Macey said defensively. "What I said was absolutely true. Besides, it's the last thing we'd have said if we were actually trying to hide something—so by saying it I made it clear we weren't hiding anything."

"Right. The next time I want to be entertained by twisted logic, I'll remember to ask you."

"And you can stop putting the blame on me, anyway," Macey went on. "You're the one who was raising red flags all over the place. You must have been grounded till you were twenty-one."

"What's that got to do with anything?"

"Because back when you were a kid and you actually pulled off a stunt, if you looked half as guilty as you did today, your parents would have locked you up."

"You're saying I looked guilty?"

"You should have seen yourself," Macey said flatly. She crossed the street to the car.

Derek closed her door and walked around to slide under the wheel. But he didn't start the engine. "That wasn't guilt you saw, Macey. That was pure horror. You have to understand that from where I was standing—"

"I know guilt when I see it. And I think the sentence you're looking for begins with *I'm sorry,* Derek."

He was incensed. "You actually expect *me* to apologize?"

Macey turned 'round in the seat to stare at him. "And why exactly wouldn't you feel it necessary? To all appearances, you don't have a general policy of never saying you're sorry, so your objection must be to apologizing for this specific incident."

"Damn right. I don't say I'm sorry unless I'm responsible, and in this case I'm not the one who caused the trouble. You, on the contrary, were scary in there."

She tipped her head back and her eyes narrowed. She looked at him for so long that Derek was beginning to think she'd faded into some kind of coma. Then, suddenly she laughed—but there wasn't much humor in the sound. "I've got it. You were actually afraid I was going to stand there in front of God and your mother and claim you— like planting a flag at the North Pole or on the top of Mount Everest."

"Well, you just came straight out with that bit about—"

"Oh, for heaven's sake. As if I'd want you. Let's get

two things straight here, Derek. There is nothing in the world that would make me consider getting married again. *Nothing.* Do you want that written in blood? Not that I'd actually do it, because I can't stand having my finger stuck. And if I ever did change my mind about that—''

He frowned. ''The finger-sticking?''

''No, the getting-married part. If I ever did change my mind about that, which I won't, the last man I'd consider marrying would be you. You're arrogant and spoiled and self-centered and conceited. If you married all six of those women, you'd have enough ego to make every last one of them regret it. I've had enough trouble just having you hanging around for the last week, so why on earth would I want to sign up for a lifetime of it?''

Her voice had risen. People on the sidewalk were veering off in a semicircle, Derek noted from the corner of his eye. They were going out of their way to avoid the car.

He didn't blame them.

Finally Macey paused for a breath, and after the silence had gone on for a few seconds, Derek said, ''Is there anything else you'd like to tell me?''

''No, I think that about covers it.'' Her voice was suddenly calm, almost friendly, fresh as the air after a sudden thunderstorm. ''Do you feel better? Because I sure do, now that we've talked this over.''

Macey caught the phone on the first ring Sunday morning, hoping that it wouldn't disturb Clara. ''Hello, Derek,'' she said as she put it to her ear.

''How did you know it was me?''

''Because no one else would be rude enough to call at this unearthly hour.''

"Did I wake you up?" His voice dripped pseudo sympathy.

She wouldn't have admitted it even if he had. Nor, for that matter, would she confess that unlike the usual Sunday morning, she'd been awake and restless for a couple of hours. "So sorry to disappoint you, but no, you didn't." She deliberately rattled the newspaper as she pushed it aside to settle down against the pile of pillows at the head of her bed with her coffee mug in her hand. "How was the Halloween party?"

"I do not understand why supposedly intelligent grownups insist on dressing up and acting like fools just because it's autumn."

"Uh-oh. Which one's off the list now?"

"Rita and Liz."

"Another two-for-one sale? You do run through them, McConnell. What happened?"

"You don't really want to know, do you?"

"Not particularly, but I thought I'd be polite and ask. In that case, I'll just cut to explaining why this is actually a positive thing and why you should be in a really good mood this morning instead of acting like the grump of the week."

"You can try explaining it to me. I'm not sure I'll believe you."

"It's because you have one name left. Only one."

"That's what you call a positive thing?"

"Of course it is. The search is over. Emily is it."

"She's the only survivor from a list that included five bad choices. That's hardly a recommendation."

"Derek, you are such a pessimist."

"After the last five, I have good reason to be edgy."

"Come on. The best part of everything always comes last. I bet she turns out to be like a tasty chocolate mousse that's served up after the overcooked pot roast and lumpy mashed potatoes are gone."

He admitted, "Even a watery chocolate mousse would look good about now."

"There's only one way to find out," Macey said cheerfully. "Go look for her. At this hour of the morning, you might even find her in a Sunday school class, teaching a bunch of little kiddies—and what better recommendation could you ask for than that?"

Derek said something under his breath and hung up on her.

Macey put the phone down. So it was going to be Emily.

Emily McConnell—it would be a nice name. Macey hoped, for Derek's sake, that Emily would turn out to be a pleasant young woman. She hoped they'd be happy together—in whatever ways each of them defined happiness.

But as for Macey herself, she mostly just felt tired. And, of course, very glad that it was over.

Macey half expected that on Monday morning Derek would be waiting for her at the office. Considering everything he'd put her through for this engagement, it seemed to her that the least he could do would be to announce it in person.

But he didn't appear, and he didn't phone. Which no doubt meant that Emily had turned out to be perfection, and Derek—in a fit of delirious relief—had entirely forgotten about Macey.

Which was just fine with her. She'd use the time to think up an appropriate gift for him and his bride.

A cappuccino machine, perhaps? The idea should have

felt funny, but it didn't. A gift certificate from a company that reorganized closets so they could hold more stuff?

Or perhaps she'd just wait a few months. There was no doubt in her mind that if Derek was cynical enough to marry to get the job he wanted, he wouldn't stop there. So sometime in the next year, there would probably be another important event to celebrate—the birth of an heir to the Kingdom of Kid. In that case, she could just combine the gifts. A lead crystal baby bottle should do the trick nicely...

Louise tapped on Macey's office door and came in. "We just got a very weird phone call," she said. Almost automatically she leaned over the one vase which was still on Macey's desk, filled with the longest-lived of all the flowers Derek had sent, and breathed deeply. "An executive secretary at McConnell Enterprises."

Macey was puzzled. "A secretary? That's odd. I wonder what Derek wants now, and why he didn't call for himself."

Louise shook her head. "It was George McConnell's secretary. She requested that we send over a temp worker for a few hours today."

Derek was already starting to pay Robert back, Macey thought. Emily must have truly turned out to be a prize. *You're glad, remember?* "What's the job? Do you think Ellen's ready to take it on?"

"She didn't give any details about the job requirements. But Ellen won't do."

"If she wasn't specific about the duties, Louise, how do you know Ellen isn't qualified? She can run just about any—"

"Oh, the secretary was specific all right, just not about the duties." Louise straightened a lily in the vase. "She wants you, Macey. Said you were the only one who'd do.'' She handed over a slip of paper. ''Here's the address. And she wants you there right away.''

By the time Derek had escaped from Emily it was after midnight, and much as he'd like to have called Macey right then, he figured that waking her up in the middle of the night to tell her exactly what he thought of the last of her six finalists wouldn't be the brightest move he'd ever made. It would be much smarter to restrain himself until Monday morning.

Of course, even if Macey yelled at him for interrupting her sleep and told him never to speak to her again, he wouldn't be much worse off.

He should have listened to his instincts, that first night at the symphony party when he'd suspected that her choice for him might be the feminine equivalent of Ira Branson. But instead he'd dismissed the feeling, telling himself that surely—with half a dozen shots at the target—she'd hit one candidate who was acceptable. After all, it only took *one*—he wasn't some kind of sheikh trying to set himself up with a harem.

Instead, a full week later he was still sitting exactly where he'd started. And Macey was going to hear about it.

His determination to catch her first thing in the morning made him restless all night, which was no doubt why he ended up oversleeping. Instead of confronting Macey at her office, he found himself rushing madly to get to his own. He was miserably late, he'd forgotten his briefcase, and he had a headache. He was also nursing a resentment the size of Boulder Dam, because he'd tried to call Macey while he was driving to work, only to be told by the receptionist at Peterson Temps that she was on the phone with an important client.

An *important* client. Implying, he supposed, that he wasn't. He didn't even leave a message, just slapped his cell phone closed.

He wasn't being fair and he knew it. He could hardly expect that she'd be reachable every instant of the day. But no matter how unreasonable it was of him, her being unavailable at the moment he wanted her only increased his aggravation level.

So he was already on a roll when he walked into the waiting room outside the executive offices to find the chairman of the board sitting there. He barely remembered to say "Good morning" to him before asking the secretary if she had an aspirin handy.

"You're having headaches fairly often these days, aren't you?" the chairman asked. "No surprise, I'd say."

"Excuse me?"

The chairman slapped his magazine shut and laid it aside. "Look, Derek, I've done as you asked and kept your confidence."

"I'm not sure I—"

"About your engagement," the chairman said impatiently.

"Oh, yes. Thank you, sir. I really appreciate your sensitivity to the—"

"But exactly who are you trying to fool here?"

Derek's blood turned to cold chunks that rattled through his veins. "Sir?"

"Friday evening when I saw you out with the blonde, I thought she must be your fiancée. So when my daughter said she'd seen you at the Halloween party with a redhead, I thought she must be mistaken. Then I thought back to what a friend said about seeing you with a brunette at the symphony party. Three different women in less than a week."

And that's not even the half of it. Derek swallowed hard.

The chairman's voice dropped, but though it was quiet it was no less chilly. "The full board meeting is coming up next week. Unless I'm satisfied with your explanation of what's going on, I will have no choice but to share this information with them. And I must warn you that not all of the directors take a worldly view of this sort of behavior."

I'm toast, Derek thought.

"And please don't expect me to believe that they were all the same woman, but she was wearing different wigs."

"I wouldn't dream of doing that, sir." *But only because I didn't think of it first—so thanks for the warning.*

The door of his father's office opened and George McConnell came out, handing a tape cassette to the secretary. "Type this letter up and get it out first thing, please. Thanks for waiting," he told the chairman. "Come on in."

The chairman stood up. "We'll finish this conversation later," he told Derek, under his breath. "I see no need for your father to be subjected to it."

At least he had a reprieve. He had a few minutes to think—if only his head wasn't pounding so badly that he couldn't.

George McConnell finally seemed to see him standing there. "You come, too, Derek—this discussion affects you as well."

There went his reprieve. Now he couldn't even call for help. And had there really been an edge to his father's voice, or was that just his guilty conscience speaking?

"Sure, Dad," he managed to say. "Just let me grab a cup of coffee and I'll be in."

* * *

But just how, Macey asked herself, did George McConnell's secretary even know her name, much less have developed the burning desire to want to work with her? Who had told her about Macey, and why had she called?

Wrong question, Macey concluded. In fact, a whole string of wrong questions. Or, to be painfully accurate, the questions themselves were sensible ones, but the person they involved was wrong. The secretary wouldn't be acting independently; she was only following orders.

Which meant it must be George McConnell who was checking out Macey.

She was still just as much in the dark about the *why,* but at least the *who* was making sense. She didn't quite see why Enid should have mentioned Macey to her husband, and why George should take the whole thing one step farther. But that must be what had happened.

Enid had seemed to accept the blithe explanation of a replacement for the crystal Derek had broken as an adequate explanation for them being seen together smack in the middle of the biggest bridal registry in town. But obviously Macey had once more underestimated Enid McConnell. Derek's mother had gone home and told Derek's father. What she'd said was anybody's guess, but it had obviously inspired George to get into the act...

Don't assume the worst, Macey told herself. *Maybe this conspiracy stuff is all in your imagination and it really is a straight temp job.*

But she couldn't make herself believe it.

She signed in at McConnell Enterprises' front desk, clipped on the visitor's badge, and followed the receptionist's directions to the corner office suite on the top floor. There another receptionist took her name and consulted someone on the phone before passing her on to the secretary whose name Louise had written down.

Macey stood before the secretary's desk, feeling very much like a student who'd just been sent to see the principal.

"Thank you for coming, Ms. Phillips," the secretary said.

"Perhaps I should explain that there's been a bit of a misunderstanding," Macey said. "I'm actually the office manager at Peterson Temps, not one of the staff. I used to go out on jobs from time to time but I don't anymore."

"I know." The secretary's voice was crisp. "Your telephone person told me."

"But then why—"

"Why are you here? I have no idea. I'm just following orders." She picked up her telephone and pressed a button. "Mr. McConnell? Ms. Phillips is here."

Macey took a deep breath and tried to brace herself.

The office door opened, and Derek came out. "Thanks for coming, Macey."

"What the—" she said.

He looked around and beckoned her across the room. "Not right now, okay? There isn't much time."

"*You* arranged this? You let me think—"

His gaze flicked toward the secretary.

Macey caught herself. "I could kick you," she muttered.

He didn't take her into the office he'd come from, but to the room next door. It was a large conference room with a long walnut table, a dozen leather chairs, and a wall full of shelves which contained enough toys to equip a day-care center, from infant rattles to tricycles, puzzles to pretend-doctor kits.

Macey took it all in at a glance as she wheeled to face

him. "What's this all about, Derek? Is it just some kooky way to announce that you got the job? Because you scared me half to death."

He shook his head. "No. Believe me, you couldn't be more wrong. You have to help me here, Macey."

"You haven't heard of *please*? What's with all the drama, anyway? Why didn't you just call me? Why haul me over here on some obviously made-up temp job?"

"I was stuck in a meeting with my father and the chairman of the board. I could hardly say, 'Excuse me, but I need to go phone the woman who's helping me pull the wool over the chairman's eyes and ask for her advice.' So I had Miranda call you. And if you need an explanation of why I didn't give her all the details..."

Macey shook her head. "No, I can see why you didn't want to explain it to the secretary. But I thought the whole thing was settled. You and Emily made an agreement, you came to work and told everybody, and now you've got the job."

"Far from it."

"Emily wasn't the answer to your prayers?"

"Please. She— Oh, never mind, it doesn't matter. There's no time for that. The chairman will be free any minute—and he wants an explanation of why I've been seen with a number of different women lately when I'm supposed to be engaged to be married."

Macey gave a low whistle. "That's not good. Though I can't say I'm surprised, because even Ira was onto that. I warned you—"

"Such a comfort you are."

"However, I'm a little lost as to what you expect me to do about it. If you think I should just start over, Derek—"

"No time for that. I need an explanation, Macey, and

I need it right now. And it wouldn't hurt if I had a name, too. Just one name—not another list.''

A name? He expected her to reach into her memory and pull out a single name? And not just any name, but the name of a woman who would meet all his criteria for a wife *and* be willing to marry him? Her mind had gone blank. Even if she'd wanted to give him a name, she couldn't have remembered one.

"I—" she began. Her voice felt wobbly.

The door opened and a big, white-haired man came in. "Well, Derek? I'll listen to your explanation now."

Derek was still looking at Macey. "That's brilliant," he whispered. He turned to face the chairman. "Sir, I didn't think a simple explanation would be enough. So I'd like to introduce you to my fiancée. This is Macey Phillips."

The blood started to roar in Macey's ears.

"She can tell you about the other women I've been seen with, too," Derek went on. "Because she's the reason I've been seeing them—she wanted me to."

CHAPTER EIGHT

DEREK thought the chairman seemed thoughtful, as if he was giving the whole idea due consideration. Macey, on the other hand, appeared to be about two inches short of murderous—and the distance was closing fast.

Uncomfortably aware that he had gambled his entire future on Macey's ability to pull herself together, Derek watched her from the corner of his eye and concluded that his best move would be to distract the chairman for a while.

He cleared his throat and said, "You see, sir, there have been at least half a dozen women in my life."

He could actually feel the vibrations of Macey's thoughts, could almost hear her saying to herself, *And that's only in the last week. Heaven knows what the real total is.*

"Of course," he went on, "Macey knows all this. We've talked about it, and I've tried to reassure her that they are entirely in the past. But the matter of these other women has continued to concern her a little."

The chairman gave a grunt. "From what I've heard about you flitting from one to another like a butterfly, I'd say she has reason for concern."

"Macey wanted to be certain—so she suggested that I see each of them one more time, keeping an open mind about their attractions and my feelings. That's why I've been flitting, as you put it—because I was anxious to satisfy her request and get back to my real choice." He smiled fondly down at her.

The chairman looked as if he'd bitten into a lemon. "Is this true, young lady? Did you actually suggest that Derek go out with women other than yourself?"

Macey swallowed hard.

Just tell the truth, sweetheart. The exact truth.

"Yes, sir." Her voice was barely audible. "I did."

Derek tried not to let his relief show.

"You actually wanted your fiancé to go out with other women? Well, that seems a mighty strange thing to me."

Macey wet her lips. "I wanted to be certain that Derek was making a decision he could live with forever. For a man who's been something of a playboy to settle down with one woman—"

"It just takes the right woman," Derek murmured.

"Marriage requires total commitment, and complete confidence between the partners." Macey's voice was gaining a little strength as she went on. "And it's much better to find out if there's a problem with that commitment before there's a wedding instead of after."

"You have nothing to worry about, darling. None of them could hold my attention for a whole evening, much less a lifetime."

She didn't seem to be listening. "Since our…engagement…"

She sounded as if she was trying not to choke on the word, Derek thought.

"…was very sudden, I thought it would be wise to take some precautions. To stop and look around before we leaped."

The chairman nodded. "I understand now, and I commend you, my dear. I hope my daughter will be as wise, when she makes her choice." He shook hands. "I'm sure I'll be seeing a great deal more of you, Miss—Phillips, was it?"

Derek held his breath, but Macey didn't correct him about the title. The last thing he needed right now was to explain why his fiancée was known as *Mrs.* Phillips.

After the chairman had gone, the silence was deafening. Macey was standing in the middle of the conference room as if she were a fashion-store mannequin who had been placed there, carefully posed, and then left to gather dust.

She was still stunned, Derek diagnosed. Well, he could sympathize with that.

Prudently, he planted himself between her and the door. "That was very good," he said. "Excellent, in fact."

She didn't answer, but at least she finally moved. Rather than trying to get around him to escape, however, she walked across the room to survey the shelves of toys and activity equipment.

"You're even better on the uptake than I hoped you would be," Derek went on. "It must be all your experience with temp jobs, but you can really roll with the punches."

Macey strolled up and down in silence, studying the shelves. Finally she stopped in front of a junior carpentry set—a workbench equipped with small scale but real tools—and picked up a hammer.

Derek eyed her warily. "Macey, that really isn't a toy. You could hurt somebody with it."

"I know." She sounded as if her teeth were gritted together. "I'm planning on it."

"Uh—Macey...."

"The only reason I rolled with the punches, as you put it, was because watching the chairman turn you into road-kill wouldn't have been nearly as much fun as doing it myself. What were you thinking of? No, let me rephrase that—because you obviously weren't thinking at all."

"When I asked you for a name, Macey, you said, 'I—' and that made me think—"

"You assumed I was volunteering?" She advanced on him.

Derek backed up a step and held both hands up, palms out. "All right—you've made your point. No, I realized you weren't talking about yourself. But still, it put the idea in my head—"

"So you're shifting the blame onto me?"

"Blame? I thought it was a great idea."

"And I suppose you also think I should fall on my knees in gratitude because I've won you as the prize in a lottery—even though I didn't have a clue I was holding a ticket. Didn't you hear me when I told you I had no intention of ever getting married again?"

"Of course I heard you," Derek said dryly. "Everybody within two blocks of that store heard you. You don't want to marry me—fine. I don't want to marry you, either."

"Then excuse me, but I don't understand what that little exercise gained you—besides a fiancée you don't want."

"That's the beauty of it, Macey. I don't know why I didn't think of it before. Now that I have a real fiancée to show off, all the pressure's gone."

"Off *you,* maybe," she muttered.

"The board's going to make their decision next week."

"And you think this pseudo engagement will satisfy them?"

"Sure, it will. They can hardly expect me to be officially married by then, since weddings do take a little time, I understand. And I'm sure you're insisting on doing the thing up right, with satin and lace and all the trimmings. No," he said heartily, "my Macey wouldn't settle for a rush job in a courtroom."

"I certainly wouldn't. As it happens, I wouldn't settle for a church ceremony either, but—"

"But as long as they don't know that, we're in great shape. Macey, they don't really want to go outside the company for the next CEO. They'd much rather give me the job, so they'll seize the excuse. And once that's settled—"

"Then the engagement's over?" There was an eager note in her voice.

He hated to squash the hope, but it wouldn't be fair to lead her on. "I'm afraid not. If a temporary engagement would have fixed the problem, I wouldn't have spent the last week trying so desperately to find someone I could marry. No, I'll still have to go through with it—but now I can take my time, look around, observe."

"It's the part about *taking your time* that I don't like."

"It'll go a lot faster when we're working together," Derek promised. "We'll make the social rounds, I'll tell you who interests me, and you can check her out. When you find someone with promise, you'll be right there beside me, so there can't be any gossip about me seeing other women behind your back."

"And when you find the right one, you'll shed me and turn up with her instead? I'm only a place-holder in the meantime?" She sounded wary.

"Well, an active place-holder—but yes."

"And when you pull off this little switch, you expect the chairman of the board not to notice?"

"Oh, he'll know it, all right, but he won't blame me. In fact, he'll probably feel sorry for me, because he already thinks you're the flighty one. With this business of wanting me to date others, it won't be any surprise at all to him when you back out. Beautiful, isn't it?''

She was looking at him with something akin to admiration in her eyes. "And you think *I'm* the expert in twisted logic? Derek, of all the incredibly insane plans—"

"Of course there's always the alternative."

"Which is?"

"We could go through with it."

She didn't even hesitate. "I'd rather be tied to a nest of fire ants and eaten alive."

Derek shrugged. "Then I guess you'll just have to play the game and help me find your replacement."

She sighed. "Let me think about it. Because in the long run it might be easier if I'd go looking for the fire ants."

Derek suggested she come along to help break the news to his father. Macey declined as politely as she could manage, reluctantly put the hammer back in place on the junior carpentry workbench, and got herself out of the building before Derek's announcement could set off some sort of fireball.

Macey thought it was quite likely. She'd tried to convince Derek to tell his father the truth about the scheme, but though he'd listened patiently to all her arguments, in the end he shook his head and said that the fewer people who knew the details, the better. Which meant, he said, that only the two of them would ever know what had really happened.

"Three," Macey corrected. "You'll tell your wife, surely."

Derek frowned.

Macey was horrified. "You can't mean you're thinking of not telling her."

"The only thing I'm thinking about is exactly why we're having this pointless conversation."

"Because if you can't tell her the truth about something like that— Oh, never mind. It's none of my business. I have to go find Clara right away, because if she finds out from your mother instead of from me, it won't be pretty."

"I hadn't thought about her," Derek admitted. "You told me she's actually your husband's aunt, right? Is she going to give you trouble about the whole idea of getting married again?"

"Probably." *Just not the sort you'd ordinarily expect.* "Derek, if I can just tell her the truth—"

But even as she said the words, Macey knew the idea would never work. Clara was a dear, but she was no conspirator. If Enid McConnell asked the right question, Clara would spill everything she knew. And no doubt Enid would have lots of questions.

So the only safe way was for Clara not to know that the engagement was only a sham until the whole thing was over. And when she found out it wasn't true after all...

"It'll break her heart," Macey said.

"I'm sorry about that."

"Not as sorry as I am," Macey muttered. "Give me a chance to find her before you start broadcasting the news, all right?"

But Clara wasn't at home. Macey waited around for a bit, but the town house felt uncomfortably empty. No— worse than empty. Most of the time, she simply didn't look at Clara's collection of photographs, but today it felt as if Jack was watching her from every wall. After a while, when Clara still hadn't appeared, Macey went back to work.

It was probably just as well if she didn't talk to Clara

for a little while, Macey tried to convince herself. She needed some time to sort this out in her own mind first. And if she couldn't find Clara, neither could Enid McConnell—so surely the news would stay under wraps for an hour or two longer.

Louise had gone out for a late lunch and Ellen was manning the reception desk when Macey came in. Macey could almost see Ellen's curiosity bubbling in her eyes.

But she wasn't about to start explaining. ''I need to get hold of my aunt,'' Macey told her, ''but I don't want to leave a message and risk alarming her. Just keep calling every fifteen minutes or so, and when she answers, buzz me.''

She went on into her office and closed the door. Not that she accomplished much except to shuffle paper, for she was still too stunned by the sudden turn of events to concentrate.

As if in a nightmare, she replayed the moment when Derek had made his announcement to the chairman of the board—and worse yet, the instant when she'd actually opened her mouth and confirmed what he'd said.

Temporary insanity, she told herself with a groan. She'd been overwhelmed by the sheer force of Derek's personality, and her own good sense had cracked under the strain.

She'd fallen into a pit full of molasses—and now she was thoroughly stuck.

Clara was in the kitchen when Macey got home, humming as she put together a stir-fry. ''Nothing fancy tonight,'' she warned. ''I'd planned a pot roast, but I was busy all afternoon.''

''I know you were out.''

Clara gave her a sideways look. ''Anyway, I didn't get

the roast started on time, so I'll fix it tomorrow. Would you chop up that onion, please?''

Almost mechanically, Macey picked up a knife.

"And how do you know I wasn't home?"

"I stopped by to talk to you. Clara—you know how I said I wasn't dating?"

"I seem to remember a conversation along those lines," Clara said dryly.

"Well, it wasn't quite true." *It wasn't false, either, but that's beside the point at the moment.* "I've been seeing someone, and….well, somehow we ended up engaged."

Clara's wooden spoon hung suspended for a moment that seemed to stretch into eons. "Oh."

"That's all you have to say about it?" Macey said finally.

"I was waiting for you to finish. *Somehow we ended up engaged* doesn't seem like a good place for the story to stop." She began to stir again. "Frankly, it sounds as if you're already having doubts about whether you've made the right choice."

No doubts at all, Clara. I'm absolutely certain I'm doing the wrong thing.

But it was a warning for Macey to be very careful about what she said. She wasn't used to Clara reading between the lines like that. Just a few months ago, when she'd still been in the depths of her depression, she wouldn't have noticed.

"You're wondering if it will upset me all over again if you move out," Clara deduced. "I'll miss you, that's sure, but—"

The front doorbell rang, and Clara put down her spoon and went to answer it. Macey pushed the chopped onion into the wok and methodically set to work reducing a green pepper to chunks.

Clara was gone for five minutes, and when she came back, she wasn't alone. "Macey, why haven't I met this young man before?"

Macey looked up in dread, but she already knew who she would see. Perhaps it was only because Clara was so tiny, but Derek looked impossibly large, looming behind her in the doorway. As if he were taking over the town house as easily as he'd commandeered her life.

"Because," Derek murmured, "Macey was afraid you'd steal my heart away from her if she let you come near me."

Clara laughed.

"What are you doing here?" Macey asked him.

"I came to meet Clara, and—now that our secret is no longer a secret—to take you to choose a ring."

"Oh, no." Macey's protest was both automatic and heartfelt, and only after it was out and she saw Derek's frown and Clara's narrowed eyes did Macey realize how it must have sounded. She scrambled for an excuse. "I mean, I think it would be much more romantic if you were to surprise me."

Clara relaxed. "That's true, you know. In my day, women never had a hand in choosing their engagement rings."

No wonder so many antique rings looked like circus jewelry, Macey thought. If the women who wore them had no say in what they looked like...

Since Derek hadn't a clue about Macey's taste, it was probably dangerous to turn him loose in a jewelry store to choose a ring for her. But it was too late to change her tactics now. Fortunately, no matter what sort of abomination he bought, she wouldn't have to wear it for long. A couple of weeks, perhaps—because surely in that length of time they could run through the entire social register.

If they went to a party or a fund-raiser or a restaurant every night...

"Dinner tomorrow," Derek was saying. For a moment, Macey thought he'd read her mind. "At my parents' house, to officially introduce the families. That includes you, Clara."

"We'd be delighted," Clara said firmly.

Macey managed to nod. So much for tomorrow's hunt for potential brides. Of course, one day more or less didn't make much difference.

"You'll stay for dinner tonight, won't you?" Clara asked.

"Thank you, but no—I have a very important purchase to make, and the jeweler is staying late to help me."

Relieved, Macey said, "Some other time, then. See you tomorrow."

Derek didn't move. "Aren't you going to walk me to the door?"

Belatedly, Macey put down her knife and led the way out of the kitchen.

"My father thinks we should entertain the board of directors, by the way."

"We?" Macey said. "Entertain? I don't suppose you're talking about a tap dance routine."

"More like dinner."

"That's what I was afraid you meant."

"The whole board only assembles about four times a year, and they travel from all over—so when they get together, they generally stay a couple of days. Dad thinks they'll want to meet you. But it doesn't have to be an elaborate thing. We could just take them to a restaurant."

Clara's head appeared in the doorway between kitchen and living room. "No, no, no. Do it yourselves. That's the only way to impress someone. It's far better to serve a very simple dish that's home-cooked than the most elaborate menu a restaurant chef can devise.'' She turned pink. "Sorry. I didn't mean to eavesdrop.'' She vanished around the corner.

"The heck she didn't,'' Macey said under her breath.

Derek lowered his voice. "Hey—she's not nearly the dragon I was expecting, from what you said.''

Macey had no intention of explaining. "Good night. See you tomorrow.'' She started to open the door.

Derek put a hand on the panel and pushed it shut. "Stop and think. If she's eavesdropping, don't you think she's going to expect to hear...other sounds?''

"Oh, please.'' But Macey had to admit he'd pegged Clara perfectly. She was capable not only of listening but of peeking around corners. Which meant that if Macey didn't kiss Derek good-night, Clara was likely to know it. Macey sighed. "I suppose I'd better get used to it.''

The corner of Derek's mouth twitched. He put his arms around her as carefully as if she were made of wax, and obediently Macey stepped closer, laid her hands on his shoulders, and turned her face up to his.

Just a kiss, she was thinking. How many times, on how many dates, had she gone through this ritual? Certainly enough that it no longer seemed important, or even meaningful. Just a good-night kiss.

And then with Jack—

Don't think about Jack right now.

She felt small and delicate, in contrast to Derek's size and solidity. She could feel the strength in his arms, and she knew that he could crush her. But she also knew that he wouldn't.

The first brush of his lips against hers was cool, almost cautious. "Oh, for heaven's sake, at least try to make it look good,'' she muttered.

Too late she saw mischief spring to life in his eyes. His arms tightened until she was pressed against him from shoulder to knee, and his kiss became the brand of a lover, teasing and tasting at first, then hot and hungry.

Involuntarily, she tensed, and he mimicked her own words, whispering against her lips. ''At least try to make it look good.''

Macey forced herself to relax. *It's only a kiss,* she told herself, but the words rang hollow. She might be vertical and fully clothed, but he was making love to her as surely as if they'd been lying together between black satin sheets...

When he finally raised his head, Macey was thinking that if she actually had been made of wax there would be no more left of her than the burned-out stub of a candle.

''We'll have to do that again,'' Derek said. His voice had a rough edge.

''I suppose so,'' Macey managed. ''I'm a bit out of practice.''

''Really? I just meant it was enough fun to be well worth repeating. But if that's what you're like when you're out of practice, I want to see what happens when you get back on the team.'' He kissed her once more, a long and lingering caress, and said, ''So what kind of ring do you want?''

Macey was having trouble breathing. ''What do I care? Choose something you can recycle.''

''That's a thought. Maybe I'll ask if I can rent one for a while. What did you have before?''

''A solitaire diamond set in yellow gold.''

''I suppose that went the way of the china.''

''You suppose right.''

He flicked a fingertip against her earlobe. ''Too bad

everybody's expecting a traditional ring, or I'd get you a pair of diamond earrings instead.''

"Too easy to lose.''

"You sure can't say that about these.''

"I like my earrings. Clara makes them for me.''

"In that case," Derek said, "you can tell her I like them too.''

And there was as much truth in that, Macey thought as she watched him cross the lawn to his car, as there was in anything else he'd said that day.

Which added up to precisely none.

The menu was the ultimate in simplicity, though it was far from easy to execute. But by late Sunday afternoon, the prime rib was roasting in the oven, the twice-baked potatoes were ready to go under the broiler for just long enough to melt the cheese on top, and the salads were already arranged on individual plates in the refrigerator. The freshly baked dinner rolls were giving off an aroma fit for the gods, and Macey was arranging a tray of appetizers while Derek finished setting up a makeshift bar on a cart just around the corner from the kitchen.

Macey set the appetizers in the refrigerator and went to give a last inspection to the dinner table. The furniture had been pushed back in the living room of the loft to accommodate the rented table, which had space enough to seat the twelve diners they were expecting. Macey thought the whole loft looked better that way—less cavernous and more homey, and in a strange way more spacious than it had before.

Derek obviously hadn't agreed, but beyond suggesting once more that they make a reservation at a restaurant instead of going to all the bother, he hadn't argued the point. And even he had admitted, once the battered surface of the table had disappeared beneath white linen and Enid's china, crystal, and silver, that it looked pretty good.

Was that a smudge on a wineglass? No, Macey decided. Just a stray reflection from the track lights above the fireplace.

"Tell me again why you think I should take a second look at Natalie," Derek said. He pushed the cart to one side and opened the glass doors to put another log on the fire.

Natalie, Macey thought absently. Now which young woman was Natalie? There had been so many.

For the last week—except for the night she and Clara had gone to the McConnells' house for dinner—Macey and Derek had partied their way across St. Louis, shopping for a suitable wife, and Macey was feeling the strain. Even tonight's dinner for the board of McConnell Enterprises looked peaceful in comparison.

Oh, yes, she remembered. Natalie was the little blonde they'd run into the night before last at the chamber orchestra. And what had been special about her? Macey tried to remember. "Because she seems nice."

Derek made a noise somewhere between a grunt and a snort.

"Come on, Derek. *Nice* might not look glamorous right now, but it would be a lot easier to live with than some other qualities I could name."

"There's such a thing as too nice."

"You don't think she was for real?" Macey straightened a salad fork and pushed a napkin back into line. "What would she have to gain from faking it?"

"I don't know. It's just a feeling."

"Well, I guess the only way to find out for sure is to marry her. You can call me in ten years and let me know which one of us was right."

"Your concern for my welfare is charming, Macey."

"That's what you're paying me for. Did I remember to tell you that my per-hour fees are triple on Sundays?"

"You remembered. I'm afraid to add it up, but I suspect your hourly rates rank right up there with the world's most exclusive courtesans."

"Really? That's quite flattering, Derek."

"But all I've gotten for it is the occasional smooch in the shadows, and then only because someone might be watching."

"Does that bother you? Here I thought the possibility of being observed just added a little illicit excitement to the whole thing," Macey murmured. "Besides, if I slept with you and you were disappointed, it would just be too awful."

"So I'm better off this way, with my idealistic dreams intact? Yeah, right. I had breakfast with my mother today."

Macey asked idly, "Your idea or hers?"

"Hers. Why?"

"Just that it's about time for her to start trying to talk you out of this. She's given you almost a whole week for the novelty to wear off, so now—"

"On the contrary. I should warn you that she's planning an engagement party."

"That's cunning of her. Can you get her to put it off?"

"Not for long. Besides, it'll be a great way for you to meet everyone on my list that we've missed so far, because they'll all be there."

"That's true," Macey said dispassionately. "I can take note of which ones are sobbing in the ladies' room at the idea of losing you."

"Mom offered to come early tonight to help."

Macey felt a jolt in the region of her solar plexus. "You didn't accept—did you?"

"No. But I wouldn't bet any money on whether she'll stay away."

"Then I'd better get changed." Macey reached for the garment bag she'd hung on a cabinet door in the kitchen and started on around the center cube to the powder room.

"You can use my bedroom," Derek said.

"I thought you—" Macey paused. "No, thanks. I'm not sharing."

"You're always looking for ulterior motives."

"That's because you generally have a few."

"Not this time. My mother's right about the size of the powder room—you couldn't maneuver yourself into a dress in there without help. Which wouldn't be a bad idea, actually, and I'd be happy to volunteer, except that there isn't room for me in there too."

"No ulterior motives, huh? If I go upstairs, I'm locking myself in the bathroom."

He held up a hand. "On my honor, Macey. I won't follow you."

She hadn't been upstairs since the day she'd rolled under his bed to escape his mother. Such a desperate and useless move that had been—though as far as Macey was aware, Enid still didn't know it had been her. Macey couldn't help but wonder who Enid thought it might have been.

She stopped halfway across the room, her breath catching in her throat. Across the muted plaid of the bedspread lay a dress.

Now I know how Enid felt when she saw the shoes, Macey thought.

But the cases couldn't be the same. No woman would have accidentally left this little number behind. It must have been deliberately left there for her to see. And Macey couldn't resist taking a closer look.

The dress was the same rich orange-red as bittersweet berries. It was long for a cocktail dress, but the modest hemline was more than balanced by the narrow straps and the deep-plunging back.

A perfect dress for the occasion. A perfect color for her, to bring out the auburn highlights in her dark brown hair. The perfect size.

And there was a note tucked into the folds of the skirt. *You told me I owed you an outfit,* it said.

She wondered who had helped him buy it.

When she came downstairs, cautious of her heels on the open ironwork of the steps, Derek was waiting. He didn't say a word, but the appreciative gleam in his eyes gave Macey goose bumps.

"Cold?" he asked.

"Just the air currents. I'll be fine."

"I can keep my arm around you all evening."

"Oh, that would be handy, trying to serve food." She looked at the clock instead of at him. "It's almost time."

"How about a kiss for luck?"

She could hardly say no. "Careful of the makeup."

"Haven't I been careful all week?" His arms were gentle, his hands soothingly warm against her bare back.

She should be used to it by now—being in his arms, being kissed. By now she should have been able to detect a pattern. But each time was new, different, unpredictable.

"You taste good," Derek whispered.

"I've been sampling the dip."

"Let me see…" He kissed her again. "Definitely not the dip. That's you."

The doorbell rang. Macey freed herself and took a quick look at her reflection in the polished brass trim on the glass doors of the fireplace. Careful or not, she looked as if she'd just been thoroughly kissed—which was no doubt exactly what Derek had had in mind. "Oh, wait," she said. "My ring—I took it off in the kitchen when I was shaping the rolls."

The ring was lying exactly where she'd left it. As she was each time she picked it up, Macey was taken aback by the sheer beauty of the enormous pear-shaped diamond and the silvery glow of the titanium band. She slipped it onto her finger, held her hand out to admire it—and only then did she actually hear what she'd said.

My ring.

But it wasn't her ring. It was only on loan to her. For all she knew, Derek might have actually talked the jeweler into letting him rent it for a while. She wouldn't blame him; though it was a ring any woman should be proud to wear, Macey couldn't see any of the beauties on his list being willing to settle for a ring that had adorned another hand, no matter how temporarily.

My ring.

How easily the words had slipped out. How easily the thought flowed through her mind.

No wonder, she mused almost dispassionately, that though she had made him lists of possible brides, she hadn't been able to feel enthusiastic about a single one of them. No wonder she hadn't been able to find one who was suitable. One whom she thought was good enough for him.

Because the fact was she wanted him for herself.

CHAPTER NINE

OF ALL the stupid moves a woman could make, Macey told herself, this one was right at the top of the heap. Falling in love with Mr. Perfection, the crown prince of the Kingdom of Kid, the guy who'd cold-bloodedly hired her to find him a wife…it had to be the most naive mistake in the history of the world.

Because, no matter how much she'd like to deny it, that was exactly what she'd done. She'd had so much fun fighting with Derek—teasing him, opposing him and annoying him—that she hadn't even noticed when fondness had sneaked into the picture, or when it had turned to affection, and then to attraction, and then to love.

Not for her the breathless adoration, the idolization, the blind devotion that was so commonly thought of as being in love. She knew Derek's every flaw, and she loved him in spite of them. Even, perhaps, because of them.

It was no wonder, she realized now, that she'd been unable to summon anything more than faint praise for a single one of the women on his list. No wonder that she'd felt so sad the day of their picnic, when she'd thought the adventure was over and she might never see him again. No wonder that she got all wobbly whenever he kissed her, no matter what the circumstances.

It was no wonder that she'd gone all domestic in wanting to have the dinner party at his loft. When she'd decided to show off her skills in the kitchen, she hadn't been thinking of impressing the members of the board—she'd been performing for Derek.

And it was no wonder she'd found herself thinking just a short while ago that this dinner party was surprisingly lacking in stress, considering the stakes. Compared to going to parties with him night after night, dinner with the board was nothing. Tonight she was not only where she wanted to be—beside him—but she would be the only woman he was watching. Tonight she could pretend that it was all real.

Or at least, that was what she would have done if this uncomfortable revelation hadn't sneaked up and kicked her in the head.

She'd believed she was safe. She had thought that her resolution never to marry again would protect her against falling in love. But somehow she'd forgotten that the two things were completely separate. She had let down her guard, and now she would pay the price.

Because when it came right down to it, nothing about the entire situation had really changed. Derek was still looking for a wife—and Macey wasn't what he was looking for. The only difference was that now she knew exactly how foolish she had been.

Derek opened the door, and George and Enid McConnell came in.

Just get through the evening, Macey ordered herself. *You can think about it all later.*

George took over the bar, and Enid ran a practiced eye over the kitchen. "I don't see how you've done it, Macey," she said. "This kitchen was obviously designed by a man who'd never cooked anything more complicated than a TV dinner."

"It's been a bit of a juggling act," Macey admitted.

The doorbell rang again.

"You've made my china look quite lovely," Enid said. "Perhaps I should just leave it here, and buy new china and silver as well as crystal. Oh, dear—how tasteless of me. Of course you'd prefer to choose your own. Perhaps we could go together sometime this week, Macey. We really need to get your patterns registered.''

Macey smiled and hoped Enid wouldn't notice that she had said neither yes nor no.

''We could take Clara and go out to lunch,'' Enid went on.

The loft began to fill. A couple of the wives joined Enid at the kitchen island. One of them cast a look around the big, sparsely furnished living room, and said, ''Well, considering it's bachelor's quarters, it's not bad. Of course you'll want a house right away—but at least we know what to get you for a wedding gift. Chairs.''

The chairman of the board was the last to arrive, well after everyone else. On his arm was a very young and very stunning blonde.

Trophy wife, Macey thought.

But the chairman introduced her as his daughter. ''Jennifer, take a lesson from this young woman,'' he said as he presented her to Macey. ''She's got some uncommonly good sense when it comes to husband-hunting.''

If you only knew, Macey thought.

''When I get ready to stalk my prey, I'll certainly call you for instruction.'' Jennifer gave a little rippling laugh.

Her warmth was infectious, and Macey couldn't help smiling back. An instant later, however, she looked past Jennifer and realized that Derek was still standing just inside the door, as if he'd closed it almost mechanically and then forgotten what to do next. His entire mind was obviously focused on watching Jennifer.

Macey felt ice start to form in her heart.

The woman was lovely. She was warm. She had a sense

of humor. And she was the chairman's daughter. How much more perfect could she be?

How odd, Macey thought, that he'd searched so desperately and so widely, only to find the woman of his dreams right at his own front door.

All evening, Macey tried not to even look in Derek's direction, for fear of what she might see in his eyes as he watched Jennifer. The young woman was the life of the party, that was sure—everyone seemed entranced with her. The men vied to draw her attention, but even the women indulged her.

In comparison, Macey felt like a lifeless frump. She toyed with her prime rib and tried not to listen to the ringing laugh coming at regular intervals from the far end of the table, almost next to Derek. Was Jennifer laughing at something he'd said?

It was hardly the most formal of dinner parties, for the layout of the loft wouldn't allow it. Macey had fleetingly considered hiring a waitress or two to serve and clear, before she realized how silly it would look to attempt such formality. In such an open space, the staff wouldn't even be able to scrape the used dishes, because every sound from the kitchen would echo.

But by the time the entrée was finished, the last trace of formality had broken down. Derek paused as he removed the plates, slung a napkin over his arm, and began to improvise a role as an uppity butler waiting table at a picnic as he finished clearing the table.

He was funny, Macey admitted, but hardly as hilarious as Jennifer seemed to find him, judging by her almost-continuous rippling laugh.

In truth, however, no one else seemed to think Jennifer was overdoing it—only Macey seemed to be disturbed.

There's nothing wrong with the girl, she told herself. *You're just upset because he's performing for her instead of for you.*

Her hands trembled a little as she served up the cheesecake for dessert. The evening was drawing to a successful close, but instead of congratulating herself she was wishing it could go on longer.

"More wine, madam?" the pseudo butler asked Jennifer with a bow.

The blonde laughed. "I'd love some. Careful what you call me, though—my daddy might not like you calling a nice girl like me a madam."

Macey gritted her teeth to keep from muttering that a truly nice girl wouldn't have drawn the connection between a term of respect and the operator of a whorehouse.

The guests lingered over coffee, but when Macey offered to refill the cups again, one of the wives laughed and said, "No, I think it's time to call the evening to a halt. I've been feeling like a voyeur for long enough."

Macey's hand slipped and she barely caught herself in time to keep hot coffee from splashing over the linen tablecloth—or far worse, over the chairman of the board. If others had noticed the intimate byplay between Derek and Jennifer...

Well, at least then they won't be surprised at the change in brides, she told herself, trying to take it philosophically.

The woman smiled at Macey. "Don't look so embarrassed, dear. You haven't done anything tasteless—in fact you and Derek haven't done anything at all to make me feel like a Peeping Tom. It's purely the way you *haven't* touched each other, or even looked at each other, that gave you away."

Macey's head was swimming.

"It's just very apparent that the two of you can't wait for all of us to disappear so you can enjoy your privacy." She set her cup down and pushed her chair back. "So though I hate to break up the party—"

Only the chairman of the board seemed to take his time in departing, but Macey admitted that perhaps Jennifer wasn't really dawdling—maybe it just seemed that way because Macey was so anxious to be rid of her.

As soon as they were gone, Macey began to transfer china from the stacks on the counter to the dishwasher, while Derek finished clearing the table. He brought the last few coffee cups out just as Macey was adding detergent.

"This thing probably hasn't worked so hard before today." She pushed the button to turn it on.

Her thoughts seemed to slosh in rhythm with the running water. *Don't even try to dodge the problem,* she thought. It would be better to bring up a painful subject herself—and try to make the mention look casual—than to have it hit her when she was even less prepared to face the question.

She wet a paper towel and began to wipe the counter. "What did you think of Jennifer?"

Derek moved the basket of rolls so she could wipe under it. "You don't ever quit, do you? I thought I told you she's the reason we're in this mess in the first place."

"You've met her before?" *And she wasn't on your list?* A trickle of relief seeped through Macey. Perhaps she'd been seeing things that weren't there. It would be no surprise if she had been feeling a twinge of jealousy, considering the shock that she had absorbed only a few minutes before Jennifer arrived.

But then why were you looking at her as if you'd been hit by lightning?

"No, I don't know her. But I had sort of had a knee-jerk reaction when her father offered to introduce me."

"And that was when you told him you were engaged—for fear his daughter would be less than compatible."

"That's the polite way to put it."

"So now that you know what he was offering, are your knees still jerking?" Macey kept her voice casual, but the effort cost her.

Derek picked up a chunk of cheesecake that had fallen onto the countertop and ate it. "You must not have heard her political views."

"No." *I was trying not to hear anything she said to you.*

"I can't even remember being that young," Derek mused. "Or that liberal, either. She's so broad-minded the wind whistles through."

"You probably never were that liberal, and you haven't been accused of being broad-minded lately, either. But being young isn't such a bad thing. You could raise her to suit you." Her conscience prodded her. *Just couldn't resist that one, could you, Phillips?*

Derek snorted. "Train her right? Not likely, with her father overseeing every move."

Macey shrugged, trying to hide her pleasure. "Well, I was just trying to do my job."

Derek stared at her. "You mean you actually would have put Jennifer on the list? Good Lord, Macey, that cheesecake must have clogged up your brain. Whoever marries her will get mighty tired of hearing about what her daddy might not like."

You should not be feeling happy about this, Macey lectured herself. *The longer it takes to find someone to suit Derek, the more painful it's going to be for you.*

And yet…in the meantime…

As long as she could keep her guilty secret hidden, she could simply enjoy being beside him. She could pretend that she belonged at his side. She could soak up the joy of being with him.

"I think that's everything." Macey tossed the paper towel away. "At least until the dishwasher finishes the first load."

"It was a knockout of an evening, Macey." He reached out, lazily, and put an arm around her shoulders. "Everybody was impressed. Including me. So, now that I don't have to be careful of the makeup anymore, I'm going to destroy it."

He was as good as his word, but he didn't stop with her makeup. He was cautious not to hurt her as he systematically ruined her upswept hairstyle, pulling out pins and dropping them at random on the floor until he could run his fingers freely through the wavy mass. Then with one hand cupped around the back of her head, he drew her close and settled to the serious business of kissing her senseless.

It took all of Macey's concentration to remember that this was more a kiss of celebration and of gratitude—and opportunity—than one of real passion. Though as it went on and the heat between them grew to nuclear proportions, she found that more and more difficult to recall.

With the last of her self-control, she put both hands against his chest. "It's late."

He sighed, and his hold loosened. "I'll take you home. Though I'd much rather not."

"You don't have to go out. I can call a cab."

"You know perfectly well that wasn't what I meant." He cupped both hands around her face and made her look at him. "Stay with me."

His voice was low and sultry, and yet there was a catch

in it. Like half-melted chocolate, Macey thought—mostly rich and creamy, but still with a lump here and there. Somehow it was even more appealing that way than if it had been entirely smooth.

"I want to make love to you, Macey." He was whispering, almost pleading.

She had expected that it might come to this, sooner or later. Pretending to be a loving couple was no big deal for a while, but if one put on a show for long enough, it was hard to escape the role. It was difficult to remember what was real and what was mere performance.

Put any normal, virile man in the situation and she suspected it wouldn't be long before he was paying more attention to physical urges than to common sense. And Derek was a perfectly normal, virile man—there was no doubt about that.

What Macey hadn't expected was that the strongest persuasion would come not from him, but from inside herself.

She had enjoyed his kisses, had even—if she was honest with herself—looked forward to them. But she had not anticipated having any difficulty in stopping the situation from going farther than kisses and caresses. She had not expected to have trouble remembering that his reaction was more to the situation than to the precise woman in his arms.

Of course, all that had been before she'd fallen in love—or at least before she'd recognized it.

That, she thought, should have made it easier to refuse—knowing that he didn't care about her at anywhere close to the same depth that she cared about him. Knowing that if it had happened to be Rita, or Liz, or Emily, or Constance—or Jennifer—in his arms, he'd have felt much the same urges.

He was kissing her again, and she suspected he was

using every seductive wile he knew. The sensual assault was taking a toll; she could feel the last ounce of objectivity beginning to slip away.

It's only one night, the little voice at the back of her brain was whispering. *What's so bad about that? Why shouldn't you have one night to remember?*

Because it was only one night, she told herself. And because one night would not satisfy—it would only feed the flames of desire.

So it's a week or two, the little voice said with a shrug. *Until he finds someone else.*

Which pretty much summarized the entire problem. Macey pulled herself together and tried to keep her voice sounding casual. "This celibacy business is killing you, isn't it?"

"It doesn't appear to be doing you any good, either," Derek pointed out. "Your skin is so hot you're practically steaming."

"Oh, you're good—no doubt about that. But that wasn't part of the deal, Derek."

His voice was rough. "So let's make it part of the deal."

If he'd slugged her she couldn't have been more taken aback. "What?"

"Let's make it real. Just leave things the way they are."

Real? Macey felt every muscle in her body contract as if it was about to go into spasm. "You mean..." Her voice cracked and she had to start over. "Surely you don't mean to suggest we get married."

Just saying the words made her ache—because asking him to deny it was too close to admitting what she wanted.

"Why not?" Derek kissed her temple, her eyelid, her cheekbone. "We've done all right together so far."

And, she could almost hear him thinking, *if we're any-where near as good in bed as it feels like we could be...*

"Look," he said, and brushed her hair back from her forehead with his lips. "I understand that you have this thing about getting married again. But this wouldn't really be like being married."

"It wouldn't?" Macey asked carefully.

"It's just a nice little affair, really. Yes, we'd have to go through the legal paperwork to satisfy everybody, but when it came right down to it—"

When it came right down to it, Macey thought, it was like being dunked in ice water.

Still....

All she had to do was say yes—and she would have what she wanted most. She would have Derek—forever. Everybody would be happy...at least more or less. Enid seemed to have warmed to the idea. Clara would be thrilled. The board of directors would be appeased. Derek would be pleased to have the whole thing settled. Even her boss would be delighted at how things had turned out and the effect it could potentially have on the temp agency.

And Macey would be ecstatic....

No, she admitted. She wouldn't be ecstatic. She wouldn't even be content for long. Unless he loved her in return, there would always be a basic inequality between them, and it would ultimately lead to insecurity, and unhappiness, and resentment.

She couldn't be satisfied with half a loaf, but that was all she would have if she married Derek. A halfway husband. A halfway marriage.

She didn't move. "So you're thinking what the hell, you have to marry somebody," she said. "Why shouldn't it be me?"

It was apparent that Derek heard the irony in her voice, for he drew a deep breath that was almost a gasp and abruptly let go of her. "I didn't say—"

"No, you didn't say it quite that way," Macey agreed. She moved away and leaned against the counter next to the dishwasher. "But it's pretty obvious what you were thinking. What happened to the idea of a new picture for the baby food jars? Had you given up that notion, or were you thinking this nice little affair would actually produce a baby?"

Derek's jaw tightened.

"And if that's the case, then exactly what is the difference between a nice little affair and a marriage? Do you intend to define it according to what's convenient for you at the moment?" She folded her arms across her chest. "No, Derek. I'm not interested."

The expression in his eyes, she thought, was a strange mixture of fascination and consternation. Too late Macey wondered if the tone of her voice had roused him to suspicion about exactly why she'd sounded sharp, almost strident.

Distract him. Try to make a joke of it.

The dishwasher went suddenly silent and then just as abruptly roared to life again, almost scaring the life out of her. But after Macey had absorbed the jolt, she welcomed the diversion. She forced a laugh. "Admit it, Derek. You're only asking me to stay because you don't want to be left with the rest of the dishes to take care of in the morning." It was lame, and she conceded the point. But perhaps it would be enough to convince him that she meant what she'd said—and absolutely nothing more.

He was very quiet for a moment. "I'll drive you home."

"I think I'd rather take a cab."

''Don't be absurd, Macey. You've made yourself clear, and I'm not about to lose my self-control. Get your coat.''

She was glad he wasn't going to make a fuss about it. Very glad.

Though she thought she might have to keep on telling herself that for a while before she actually believed it.

The directors' meetings alternated between McConnell Enterprises' many locations, so it had been well over a year since all the directors had been gathered at headquarters. On Monday morning, Derek gave them all a tour of the newest production line, which was currently building bright-colored, kid-size bookcases and bins from pellets of recycled plastic, and he patiently answered questions about new products and marketing and sales for more than an hour.

Then they had a buffet lunch at the country club followed by eighteen holes of golf, and Derek had no sooner hit a long drive off the first tee than he found himself wishing he was back in the plant. At least there, the questions had been clear and direct—and he'd known the answers.

On the golf course everything was less explicit. Nobody came straight out and asked when his wedding would take place, but there were hints and allusions and references aplenty.

He hadn't anticipated that the subject would be of such overwhelming interest to a bunch of middle-aged men. And though he'd been perfectly prepared to deal with generalities, he was completely taken off guard by the jokes. Jokes about weddings, jokes about newlyweds, jokes about babies. Funny stories, foolish stories, tasteless stories.

But all of them had one thing in common—an undercurrent of approval. They liked Macey. And tomorrow, when they voted to make him CEO, and asked exactly when he planned to marry Macey...

Derek shot his worst round in a year, made excuses that sounded lame even to him in order to escape the shot-by-shot postmortem in the bar, and sat in his car stalled in rush-hour traffic trying to figure out what to do. All his options seemed to circle around and around and come inevitably back to the center, like water swirling 'round a basin before it trickled down the drain.

Which—at the moment—was a pretty apt description of the situation he was caught in.

It was Clara who answered the door, and Derek, unsure of what Macey might have told her, braced himself, because he half expected to be told to go away. But Clara merely eyed the long white box he carried and said, in the same friendly manner she'd always used toward him, that Macey wasn't home from work yet.

"I thought she made it a point not to work evenings and weekends," Derek said, before he stopped to think.

"She did—until she met you," Clara said crisply. "Now she's having some trouble keeping up. Come on in and I'll make you a cup of tea."

A stiff Scotch on the rocks sounded more inviting, but Derek wasn't about to turn Clara down. At least he was inside the door, and he suspected that was farther than he'd have gotten if Macey had been at home to greet him.

He started to follow Clara to the kitchen, but she waved him to a seat on the couch. "I'm cleaning out cupboards," she said. "There's no place even to lean."

He was too restless to sit, so he wandered around the living room instead.

He hadn't spent much time in Macey's living room.

Mostly he'd just walked through it to get to the kitchen—
except for the night he'd first kissed her, and on that occasion the only part of the decor he'd been interested in
had been Macey herself.

The room was comfortable rather than elegant, with an
odd mixture of furniture—ranging from a Mission-style
sofa table to a Victorian velvet side chair—that somehow
managed to look as if it belonged together. On the sofa
table and above it on the wall was a lineup of picture
frames. Idly, he glanced at them, and then took a closer
look.

There were a few pictures of Macey—one a formal
pose in a wedding gown, another a snapshot which included a thin, sickly looking young man.

The husband, he deduced. What was his name? He
knew he'd heard it, but he couldn't remember.

The rest of the photos were of the young man alone,
but there was another difference as well—he was lively,
healthy, smiling. With a tennis racquet, in a business suit,
leaning against a classic Corvette. It was too bad that
Macey had no doubt had to sell the car, too, since it was
probably worth twice as much now.

Clara came in quietly, carrying a tray. "That's Jack,"
she said. "Though I don't guess I need to tell you that."

Derek cleared a spot on the coffee table for the tray she
carried. Clara filled a teacup for him, then settled back in
the velvet chair with her own cup and looked at him ex-
pectantly. "You have a problem," she said finally.

Was it that obvious? *As a matter of fact,* he wanted to
say. *I need to convince Macey to marry me. Can you
help?*

But of course he couldn't say anything of the sort. Clara
thought the engagement was real, so if he admitted it

wasn't, he might as well go stand in the middle of the freeway and wait for a truck to hit him.

"Have you and Macey had a quarrel?"

At least that he could answer—though it would still be wise to weigh his words carefully. "Not a quarrel, exactly. More like a disagreement."

"And you've brought flowers." She pointed at the long white box. "That's a good start. I'll excuse myself, of course, as soon as she comes home. Unless there's something else I can do to help—"

"You're not unhappy? About Macey and me, I mean." *You liar,* his conscience whispered. *There is no Macey-and-me.*

"On the contrary. I'm relieved that Macey has finally stopped mourning Jack and picked up her life again." She sipped her tea. "I helped my brother raise Jack. He was like a son to me—the only family I had after his father died—and when I lost Jack too, I took it very hard. But Macey thought her life was over, and that has worried me a great deal. She's far too young to be so solemn about never wanting to marry again."

But Clara didn't know the truth, Derek reminded himself. All the changes she was celebrating existed only because of the part Macey was playing.

"Of course, that was all before she met you." She smiled. "It would take a pretty special guy to convince Macey she'd been wrong."

Yeah, Derek thought. *Trying to change Macey's mind is like requesting the faces on Mt. Rushmore to look the other direction for a while.*

"She's been very brave, through everything," Clara went on. "That's why I'm so happy that she's finally moved on."

But the truth was Macey hadn't moved on, Derek

thought. From his seat on the couch he could see at least twenty photos of Jack. And how many reminders of her marriage—symbols of her vanished happiness—didn't he recognize? The sofa table, perhaps? Or the pillow he was leaning against?

And he had blithely—foolishly—lightly suggested that she marry him. He had made it sound like some kind of prank.

You should be locked up for your own protection, McConnell.

The back door banged, and Derek winced at the sound. "I think she must have seen my car."

Clara nodded and set her cup down. "I'll just go up to my bedroom."

Macey appeared in the doorway between kitchen and living room, her coat still on, her hands dug deep into the pockets.

Derek stood up. "I came to tell you I'm sorry about last night. I didn't handle that very well." He held out the long white box.

Macey didn't take it. She didn't even move from the doorway. "You're on your own tonight, Derek. I have a pile of paperwork to get through."

"You think I came to talk you into going to another party?"

"Isn't that why you're here? You still need a wife."

"Yes," he said very quietly. "I do. Macey—please listen. I made a mess of it last night."

"You certainly did."

Somehow, that quiet statement gave him hope. He'd messed it up, yes—but surely he could still fix it. "Will you think about what I asked you? I don't want to push you—but I really need you to consider it."

"I suppose that means the board is pressuring you for a wedding date."

He tried to smile. "The trouble is, you did too good a job with that dinner party last night."

She moved finally, but only to take off her coat and drape it across Clara's chair. "So your being stuck is *my* fault?"

"No. Of course not. Please, Macey—I've got myself in a hole."

"What's new about that? Anyone with half a brain could have seen it coming. You deserve it."

"The formal vote is tomorrow. But before they offer me the job, they're going to want to know my plans."

"So what are your plans, Derek?"

He said, very quietly, "I want you to marry me."

The words seemed to echo around her. For a moment, Macey let herself feel, and think, and hope, that it was real. That he meant what he'd said. That he truly wanted not just to get married, but to marry her.

Then she sighed and said, "Give me one reason why I should find that proposition any more inviting than I did last night."

Please, a little voice deep inside her whispered. *If you can't tell me you love me, that's all right. If you can just tell me you care a little...*

"I know you had a difficult time, with Jack's illness and the bills and everything," he said softly.

"You have no idea."

"It wouldn't be like that again. I can make it easy for you."

She said slowly, "So this is about money? That's what you're offering?"

"You're twisting things, Macey. I desperately need you."

She half turned toward him, afraid to believe what she'd heard.

"Last night I was cocky and rude, and I made you angry. It wasn't very respectful of me to joke about making it an affair. So—you set the rules, Macey. Our marriage will be whatever you want. Any conditions you set, I'll agree to."

She let the silence stretch out, waiting and hoping. But there was nothing more.

"Why so flexible all of a sudden?" she asked finally. "Because now that the board's actually met me, only I will satisfy them?" She saw the answer flicker in his eyes, and if he'd stabbed her it couldn't have hurt worse. "Well, you're just going to have to deal with that—without my help."

"Macey, please—"

She wheeled to face him. "No. I will not marry you. So what's your next plan? Because if you're thinking of asking me to pick up where we left off and keep looking for some willing guinea pig, you can think of something else. I should have called a halt to this childish stunt a long time ago. In fact, I should never have agreed to get involved in the first place. But no more, Derek. I am not going to be a part of it anymore, watching you cheat and lie and manipulate the system to get what you want, no matter what it costs other people. I'm done with this— and I'm done with you."

The sudden attack had shocked him into silence, that was obvious. The color had drained from his face, but he wasn't just pale—his skin actually seemed to have turned a sickly shade of gray.

Good, Macey thought. At least she'd managed to stun

him back to reality. Obviously he was so used to getting his way that he seemed to think it was his right—but she'd managed to clear up that misapprehension, and none too soon. He looked as if he'd never been told *no* so sternly in his life.

"If you're quite finished with your analysis of my character," he said, "then consider yourself relieved of duty."

Macey hadn't thought it was possible for her to feel angrier, but that did it. "You can't fire me, because I've already quit!"

"Call it whatever you wish." Derek's voice was quiet. "I'll take it from here." He closed the door behind him with a soft click which was brutally final.

Macey stood in the center of the room for a couple of minutes, listening to the silence. Then she picked up the long white box and carried it to the kitchen to put it in the garbage.

CHAPTER TEN

MACEY dumped the box on top of a cantaloupe rind and a heap of coffee grounds and squashed it down so the wastebasket would still fit under the sink. Clara walked in just as Macey was pushing it back into place.

"What kind of flowers did Derek bring you?" she asked brightly.

"I don't know."

Clara's forehead wrinkled. "But you just put the box in the garbage."

"Yes—I did. I have a headache, Clara. If you'll excuse me, I'm going to spend the evening in my room." Macey thought Clara might argue, or ask for explanations. But the old woman didn't say another word.

Macey carried her stack of folders upstairs with her, but she didn't turn the lights on in her bedroom. She hadn't been exaggerating the headache, and the very idea of bright light and fine print made the pain throb even worse. She lay down on the bed and stared at the ceiling.

She had done the only thing she could.

Looking back on the discussion, she thought that it might perhaps have been wiser not to go into quite so much detail about what she saw as Derek's shortcomings. But at that moment it had appeared that nothing less would have convinced him that she meant what she said. In any case, it was done now.

It was all done. Over. Finished.

Until tonight, she had still felt a glimmer of hope. Even though she had told herself it was impossible Derek could care about her the way she cared about him, somewhere deep inside she had still cherished the possibility. Even while she denied it, she had dreamed. But tonight that illusion had flickered like a guttering candle and finally gone out.

She felt empty.

For so long, she had been only half alive. Then, despite herself, Derek had awakened her once more—only to end up by proving she'd been right in the first place. Right to depend only on herself. Right not to trust. Right not to take the chance of being abandoned again.

She didn't blame him exactly, for heaven knew he hadn't done it on purpose. He hadn't led her on, or made promises. In fact, he'd been brutally honest from the start about his intentions. It was Macey's own fault that she had dismissed the facts and looked instead at the fantasy figure she'd created.

Despite everything he'd said and done, she had believed that deep down inside he was a romantic. She had concluded that he was unable to settle on a logical choice for a wife because the emotional side of him longed to find the one special woman who could make his life complete. And she'd foolishly allowed herself to hope that she might be that woman.

She'd been wrong. Instead of being a starry-eyed dreamer in search of love, he was a perfectionist and a fussbudget. No wonder he'd been finding fault with every woman who crossed his path—he was impossible to please.

She wondered what he'd do now. Draw a name out of a hat? Pity the poor woman who came up the loser in that lottery.

Not that it would make any difference to Macey. Most

likely, she'd never even know whether it was Liz he married, or Emily, or Rita, or Constance...

As her eyes grew accustomed to the dim glow which filtered through the curtains from the streetlights outside, Macey noticed the dress she had worn for the dinner party. It was hanging on the back of the closet door, waiting to go to the cleaner's.

What a perfectly apt, melancholy, heart-breaking shade of red it was, the color they called bittersweet....

It hurt too much to think about, but she didn't have the energy to get up and put the dress out of sight. She looked around her bedroom instead, seeking something else to concentrate on.

When she'd first moved into Clara's guest room, she'd been too numb to think about redecorating it as her own. Then she'd been too busy, too concerned with her job and with Clara's illness. But now, with her finances finally straightened out and Clara feeling better, she might consider finding an apartment for herself. Somewhere she could make into a home just for her.

For it was darned sure she was going to be on her own.

Derek had turned his desk chair to the window and was staring out. In the distance, under a gloomy October sky that promised rain later in the day, he could see the stainless-steel Gateway Arch looming over downtown St. Louis. Today, with no brilliant sunshine to reflect, it looked as dull as a worn-out mirror. Just about the same way he felt, now that he'd finished sorting through all his options and he'd come to a decision.

He turned his head at a tap on the office door, and George McConnell came in. "The board's all here," he said. "They're in the conference room chowing down doughnuts and coffee."

"I'll be there when the meeting starts."

"You'd better come in now and do a little last-minute politicking."

"In a minute."

"Derek, don't count on having this thing won." George laid a hand on Derek's shoulder. "I get the feeling there are still some doubts—they just haven't been expressed openly. If you're acting aloof, you'll just give those guys a reason to wonder about you."

He was right, Derek knew. He reached up and put his hand on top of his father's. "I understand, Dad. Thanks."

George wrinkled his brows as if he'd like to ask for an explanation, but he didn't press. He closed the door behind him.

Derek sat still a little longer, thinking. Then he stood up, took a deep breath and let it out, and put on the suit jacket he'd discarded earlier. He stopped beside his secretary's desk to sign a couple of letters, knowing full well that he was purposely dawdling. But finally there were no more excuses for delaying.

The board members were settling themselves at the long conference table when he came in. There were still trays of doughnuts, but he shook his head when his father gestured him in that direction. Instead he took his regular seat near the foot of the table, where he could see the row of shelves full of their products—including the junior carpentry set which contained the hammer Macey had used to threaten him.

The chairman called the meeting to order, and Derek let his mind wander while they proceeded through the usual formalities. Then the chairman said, "The next order of business is to decide the procedure the board will follow in hiring a new chief executive officer." He looked over his half-glasses at Derek. "You're an *ex officio* member of this board, so we can't require you to excuse your-self from this discussion. However—''

Derek stood up. ''In order to allow a frank and open discussion, I will of course leave the room. But first, gen-tlemen, I have an announcement to make.''

Macey usually enjoyed talking to Peterson Temp's work-ers when they came back to the office after completing a job, especially when it had been the worker's first assign-ment. The debriefing process was usually enlightening, frequently making it easier in the future to match workers with the company. And most of the time, it was just plain fun to listen to a worker who had successfully completed an assignment—especially one like Ellen, who had gone out with so many doubts about herself and returned with so much more confidence that she hardly seemed like the same person.

Nevertheless, today Macey was having trouble concen-trating. It had been just thirty-six hours since Derek had walked out of the town house, and Macey had been suf-fering pangs of regret for at least thirty-five of them.

She knew she had made the only decision she could. She knew that accepting his proposal would have taken a horrible toll on her self-esteem, and that it was a price she could not afford to pay.

Nevertheless, part of her wished that she had said yes instead of no.

Perhaps, whispered a wistful little voice in the back of her mind, *just perhaps he would have learned to love you, if you had only given him—and yourself—the opportunity.*

''Not a chance,'' she said firmly. That was only wishful thinking, and it would lead her precisely nowhere.

Ellen looked startled. ''Excuse me? But—why won't you let me try a longer assignment next time?''

Macey tried to pull herself together. "Ellen, I'm sorry. I was...my mind had drifted. You were saying...?"

She had awakened at dawn that morning to the sound of the garbage truck pulling away from the house, and that was when the twinges of regret had become sharp, shooting anguish—for the garbage collectors were taking away the last thing Derek had given her.

Until the moment when the garbage truck roared away down the street, she'd almost made herself forget about the long white box. She'd kept herself too busy to think. It was only when it was too late to retrieve it that she realized what she'd done.

She didn't even know for sure what the box had contained. Flowers, Clara had said—and she had probably guessed right.

Of course, Macey reminded herself, even if she had kept them, flowers would be gone in a matter of days, wilted and faded and musty. Perhaps it was better to cherish the idea of a dozen roses than to have tried to hold on to the reality.

And perhaps it hadn't been a dozen roses at all, but something more along the lines of stinkweed....

No, that was what he'd be likely to send her now—if he felt some overwhelming need to send her anything at all. Which he wouldn't, of course. There was no reason for him to be in contact ever again.

And no reason for her to feel as if the world had jolted to a halt because Derek McConnell wasn't coming around anymore.

Mechanically, she finished Ellen's assessment. "You can check with Louise about another assignment," Macey told her. "After two or three—or whenever you're comfortable—you won't need to come in to the office to report each time. Then you'll just phone in on the last day of a job, and Louise will tell you about the next one.''

When Ellen opened Macey's office door, Robert was just raising his hand to knock. ''Oh, good, you're free,'' he told Macey. ''Terrific news—but why hadn't you told me?''

''News?'' she asked warily. ''I'm not sure what you mean.''

''Oh, come on, Macey. About Derek.''

It would be just her luck, Macey thought, if after she'd spent an entire week doing a mental balancing act every minute of every day, Robert was just now hearing the rumor of her engagement. For a solid week it seemed she'd thought of nothing else—trying to keep straight who knew, who had yet to be convinced, and who was to be kept in the dark.

She had deliberately not mentioned it to anyone at Peterson Temps. She had deliberately not worn Derek's ring anywhere near the office, just so she wouldn't have to answer questions. But now—two days after her fake engagement was over—her boss had finally heard about it.

It was enough to make a woman shriek.

And even if that wasn't enough to cause hysteria, she realized, the very thought of the ring was.

She hadn't been wearing the ring on the night Derek had actually proposed—the night she'd turned him down for the final time. She had just come from work when she'd found him waiting for her, and the ring had been safely tucked away in the bottom of an old purse in her closet.

Where it was still lying, forgotten—until this moment—in the dark.

* * *

Louise returned from her lunch break with a sandwich for Macey, who took it into the computer lab just for a change of scenery. While she ate, she idly paged through a newspaper that someone had left lying there, and in the business section she saw what Robert had been talking about this morning. It hadn't been her pseudo engagement he'd been reacting to, she realized. It was the announcement that the board of directors of McConnell Enterprises had named their next CEO.

Derek had gotten the job.

It seemed he was a magician of note after all, Macey thought, if he could pull that rabbit out of the hat. She wondered how he'd managed to make her vanish so neatly that the board seemed to have entirely forgotten her existence. Smoke and mirrors? Or had he used the old saw-the-girl-in-half trick?

And who had he put in her place?

As if it ever was your place, she mocked herself.

The news complicated matters for Macey, however, because she still had to return his ring. It wasn't the kind of thing she felt like trusting to a messenger, yet she certainly didn't want to do it herself. Not only didn't she want to face him, but having her turn up in person was probably the last thing Derek wanted, too.

Since she had no idea what he'd told the board—or even his parents—about the breakup of his supposed engagement, she could hardly pay a call at his office. If, for instance, he'd told them that she'd abruptly moved to Paris, or that she'd broken both legs and landed in the hospital in traction, or that she'd been arrested and thrown in jail because she'd been blackmailing him into pretending they were engaged....

No. No matter how he'd explained the sudden breakup,

she didn't want to face him in public. But she *really* didn't want to seek him out in private.

Her entire body hurt at the very idea.

Ted the doorman looked from Macey to the pizza box and back. "Mr. McConnell didn't say anything about you coming by."

"I'm not surprised. He wasn't expecting me." She thought she saw him sniff, and she tried to unobtrusively waft the scent of pepperoni in his direction. "Is he at home?"

Ted shook his head. "He went out a little while ago. Didn't say where he was going. Maybe to his mother's for dinner, because she was here earlier."

A family dinner with the new fiancée, no doubt. I wish the poor woman good luck.

"Oh." Macey tried to look disappointed. "Then he won't be back for hours, I suppose." She set the pizza box down on the doorman's stand, next to Ted's elbow.

There was no doubt about it this time; he inhaled deeply.

"Look," she said, lowering her voice. "I just wanted to drop off something for him. A silly little thing."

"Leave it with me and I'll give it to him the minute he comes in."

Oops. This wasn't going at all the direction she'd hoped. "It wouldn't be the same, Ted. Exactly where I leave it is as much a part of the message as the thing itself. It's silly, but you know how it goes. You have a key to his loft, don't you? You must have. Look, you can stand right outside the door. One minute, that's all it'll take."

"Yeah," he muttered, "like any woman on earth actually knows how long one minute is. Twenty would probably be more like it. This thing you're leaving isn't full of explosives, is it?''

He was weakening. ''Do I have reason to want to blow him up?'' Macey opened the small bag she was carrying. ''Look. It's completely innocent.''

Ted took the small stuffed skunk she handed him, turned it upside down, squeezed it, sniffed it, and handed it back. ''Okay,'' he said finally. ''I'll let you in, and you lock the door on your way out. I'm not standing there waiting for you.''

Even better than I hoped. ''Deal,'' Macey said. ''You don't mind if I leave this pizza with you, do you? I'm not nearly as hungry as I thought I was.''

Ted rolled his eyes and didn't answer.

He let her into the loft and pulled the door closed behind her. As the latch clicked, Macey stood just inside the door for a long moment and looked around.

The table and chairs they'd rented for the dinner party were gone. Enid's china was either stashed away in a closet, or she'd taken it home. The couch had been pulled back into place in solitary splendor. The kitchen once more looked as if it had never been used. The quiet was intense.

She reached into her pocket and pulled out the engagement ring and a length of white ribbon. She tied the ribbon in a floppy bow around the neck of the stuffed skunk, tied the ring to the ribbon, and tried to decide where to leave it so he'd be sure to see it. The kitchen counter? The mantel? Not so good if he brought the fiancée home with him.

On his pillow?

Macey had to bite back a smile at the idea of the new fiancée discovering a stuffed skunk wearing an engagement ring on Derek's pillow. Now that was truly an inspired idea.

Still, even though she strongly disapproved of what he was doing, Macey was determined not to deliberately cause trouble. It was going to be difficult enough for this couple to make things work without any help from outside to make things worse.

The coffee table, she decided, was the least personal, least intrusive spot, and yet—since the couch was the only spot to sit—he'd be bound to see it almost as soon as he came home.

She walked across the room and stopped dead in the center of the room. On the coffee table, as if it had been carelessly tossed there, was a long white box.

A long white box, still taped shut, stained brown and orange all along one end. Stained by coffee and cantaloupe from when she'd shoved it into the wastebasket in Clara's town house.

She reached out a hand and then drew it back as if the box might burn her.

It's yours, part of her whispered. *He gave it to you.*

But you threw it away, her conscience replied. *So even if it did belong to you once, it doesn't anymore.*

A key clicked in the lock. Macey's heart jolted violently and then settled back into place. *It's Ted,* she thought. He must have come upstairs to remind her that her one minute was long gone.

The door swung open and Derek came in. He tossed his car keys on the kitchen island, stripped off his leather jacket, and crossed the living room toward her.

He looked very tall, very strong, very powerful—and not at all startled to see her.

"Ted told me you went out for the evening," she said, feeling as foolish as she must sound.

"I did go out. He called to tell me I had a visitor, so of course like a good host I came straight home."

She was incensed. "He called you? That no-good little—"

"You of all people shouldn't be surprised, Macey. I took your advice after my mother walked in on us that day."

She should have expected it. "You increased his bribe?"

Derek nodded. "When it comes to buying loyalty, a pepperoni pizza isn't even in the same galaxy. So what brings you here?"

She picked up the little skunk and held it out.

His eyebrows raised. "Another comment on my character?"

"No! I meant… I felt bad about forgetting to return your ring. It's…" She fumbled with the ribbon, loosened the knot, and released the ring. "Here. I meant it to say that I felt like a skunk for not giving it back. I just forgot." She was babbling, but she couldn't stop herself.

"You forgot?"

"Well, it wasn't like I meant to keep it," she said defensively. "The skunk was supposed to be funny."

He didn't smile. And he didn't seem to notice that she was holding the ring out to him.

The metal band felt so hot she couldn't hold it any longer. She reached for his hand, turned it, and dropped the ring into his palm. "I'm sorry. I only meant to return the ring in a way that wouldn't hurt either of us. I'll go away now."

His fingers tightened on hers for an instant—or was it only her imagination?—and then let her hand slip away.

Slowly she walked across the room. But she couldn't just leave; she had to know. "Derek? What's in the box?"

For a moment she thought he wasn't going to answer at all. "You had your chance to find out, Macey."

"Yeah," she said softly. "I really blew it, didn't I?" She was putting her hand on the doorknob when he turned to face her.

"I got the job," he said abruptly.

"I know. I saw it in the newspaper." She tried to put a little liveliness into her voice. "Sorry I forgot to congratulate you—I was a little preoccupied when you first came in."

"You were wondering how the box got here," he said. "Because the last time you saw it, it was in a wastebasket."

There was no point in trying to hide the facts. "Well—yes. I did wonder. Not that it's any of my business."

"Clara rescued it from the garbage and gave it to my mother today at their porcelain painting class."

"Your mother's taking porcelain painting too?"

"And Mom brought it by on her way home."

"But neither of them opened it? That's next door to superhuman."

He moved a little closer. "You didn't open it, either."

"That was different." Uneasily, she fumbled for a change of subject. "When's the wedding, Derek? And who's the lucky woman? Jennifer? She's the only one I can think of who could have won such quick approval from—"

"There isn't going to be a wedding."

Macey frowned. "But—you got the job. How— You're not still trying to convince them that *I'm*—"

"No." His voice was unusually deep. "I thought over what you'd said, and what I was trying to do. And in the end I told them the truth—that there isn't going to be a wedding."

"You confessed to the board that you'd made it all up? And they hired you anyway?" Macey shook her head in disbelief. "Well, if that isn't a kick in the pants. All that work, all that effort, all those damned parties we went to, for nothing?"

"It wasn't quite that smooth or easy. I admitted that I had tried to fix the odds, that I had every intention of marrying just to get the job and that I didn't much care who I married." His voice had softened until she had to lean closer to hear clearly. "And I told them that when it came right down to it, I couldn't go through with the plan."

She had thought she'd rooted out every last fragment of hope, but a few leftovers must have been crouching in the back corners of her mind, for now they crept forward into the light. "Why?" She could manage nothing more than a whisper.

"Because it would have been cheating—and in the end nobody would have been happy. Not the board, not the company, not me, and certainly not the woman I had married for all the wrong reasons."

But not because of you, Macey. The feeble fragment of hope retreated into the darkness.

"I told them they had to make a choice," Derek went on.

"To give you the job anyway, or—" She couldn't think of an alternative. "What?"

He shook his head. "No. I told them I would stay on at McConnell Enterprises if they wanted to keep me in my current job. Or if they'd rather, I would leave when the new CEO came on board, so he'd have a free hand."

Macey was aghast. "Derek, that's got to be the world's biggest bluff. What if they hadn't taken you seriously?"

"I wasn't bluffing, Macey." He put a fingertip under her chin and nudged her jaw back into place.

"You'd have given up your job? Left your father's company?"

"Yes—I would have." He looked down at the ring, still gleaming in his palm, and set it carefully on the kitchen island next to his car keys.

He was treating it with such care because it was valuable, Macey told herself. Not because it was important to him in any other way. He probably couldn't wait to take it back to the jeweler so he could be rid of it—and the bill.

She had to get away. But her feet seemed to be glued to the floor.

"You can open the box if you want, Macey."

She was afraid to open it. Afraid to see what was inside. But if she refused, then she had no excuse to stay longer. And though part of her yearned to go, the other part couldn't bear to leave.

She worked a fingernail under the edge of the tape to loosen it, and the top of the box tore as the flap finally came loose.

Inside, nested in layers of tissue paper, was the Lalique vase he had considered buying for his mother, until Macey had told him it wouldn't be the right gift for Enid. The one Macey had admired for herself.

"It's beautiful," she whispered. But he had said she could open the box, not that it was hers. Her fingertips seemed to cling to the cool glass, and it took effort to let it slide back into the box. "Thank you for letting me see it." She held the box out to him.

He didn't move to take it. "But you already have a thousand vases, right?"

"Not like this one," she said softly. *Nothing could be like this one—because you chose it for me.*

"When Mom brought it back, I went out to find you. That's what I was doing when Ted phoned."

Macey frowned. "You were looking for me? Why?"

"To make you accept the vase. Only I was in such a hurry I forgot to take the vase with me."

"That doesn't make any sense."

"Neither does anything else I've done lately." He sounded almost sad. "What you said to me that night made me think, Macey."

"It was intended to," she said dryly.

"You were right. I was trying to manipulate the system. I thought I'd figured out a way to play the game without following the rules. And it wasn't until that night, when you made me step back and look at the mess I'd created, that I realized I'd gotten myself caught in a snare, and you were the only answer."

She took a step toward the door. "There's really no point in going over this ground again, Derek. Now that you have your job settled—"

"This has nothing to do with my job. And I'm not finished. It was only when you turned me down that I realized what was happening. Though I suppose I should have known the day you told me your husband had died."

"You should have known what?" she asked carefully.

"Because when you said that, it was like you'd hit me right in the gut with a baseball bat. I thought at the time that I felt bad because of what I'd just been saying to you—giving you a hard time about not telling me, stuff like that."

"It *was* pretty tasteless of you."

"Don't rub it in. It was only later—a long time later—

when I realized that the reason I felt so bad was that I felt guilty about feeling good.''

Macey put her fingertips to her temples. "I don't begin to understand what you're talking about.''

"I wasn't happy that he was dead. But I sure was pleased to find out that you were free after all.''

"So I could still lend you a hand. What's new about—''

"No,'' he said. "Though that's what I thought at the time. The whole idea of double dating wasn't to provide cover while I got to know those six women you'd chosen. It was only an excuse to see you.''

She was suddenly breathless with hope—and with fear that the sudden stirring of optimism would once more be crushed into dust.

"You'd done what I asked—you'd given me the list of finalists. Your job was finished. But I didn't want to let go of you. That's why I leaped on the excuse to announce that you were my fiancée—because I wanted you to be. And that's why I told the board that there won't be a wedding. Because only you will do.'' He glanced at her and then looked away again. "Macey, I know you said you'd never get married again. And I know I could never be what Jack was to you. But—''

Macey said quietly, "I wouldn't want you to try.''

He took a deep breath, and released it slowly. It sounded harsh in the quiet loft. "Well, that's pretty plain. I won't bring it up again.'' He moved to open the door for her.

Macey stayed rooted to the spot. "When Jack first got sick—before we knew how serious it was—I was almost glad. It explained so much, you see. If he was ill, that's why he'd been so tired and so short-tempered. That was why he didn't seem to want to go anywhere or to do anything with me. That was why he didn't seem to find me attractive anymore.''

Derek stopped with his hand on the doorknob. ''He had a brain tumor, right? And it messed up his thinking?''

She smiled a little. ''No brain tumor. He had a girl-friend—but she had pretty much the same effect on the thinking. I found out about her the first time he was in the hospital. I'd gone home to rest, couldn't sleep, went back to his room. And there she was.''

Derek swore under his breath.

''It was the next day the doctors told us that he had only a few months to live.''

''And then he swore he'd give her up and begged you not to leave him?''

''No, he didn't,'' Macey said coolly. ''He made it quite clear that we were both welcome at his bedside, and if either of us objected to sharing, that was our problem, not his. And since the girlfriend—''

''You mean The Tumor?''

''That's a good name for her. Since The Tumor had known about me all along, she was quite content to share. Especially the parts that weren't much fun.''

''You actually stayed with him after that?''

''You're thinking I should have created a scene and walked out? Maybe I should have. But I was too shocked to do anything. One week I was reasonably happy, just bumping along, telling myself that every marriage has its problems from time to time. And then the next week my husband was dying and my marriage was dead. Besides, there was Clara. She was losing her favorite nephew—the only family she had left.''

''She told me once that she helped raise him.''

Macey nodded. ''I couldn't bring myself to destroy her image of him.''

"It wouldn't have been your fault. It was his."

"Yes—and perhaps I would have told her sooner or later. But the few months the doctors expected him to have, turned out to be only a couple of weeks instead. So I thought, why tear Clara up? He was gone. Why not let her keep her vision of him as this wonderful young man?"

"The pictures," Derek said suddenly. "Why are the pictures all over your house?"

"They're Clara's. It's her town house—I moved in after he died."

"Oh, yes—you told me that once. So that's why you sold your engagement ring, and the china. You didn't want the reminders."

"They weren't exactly sentimental souvenirs—but I truly did need the money."

"And his Corvette—"

She shook her head. "I didn't sell the car. I didn't find out till after he died that he'd signed it over to The Tumor just a few days before."

"She got the car, and you got the bills?"

"Sharing is such a wonderful thing," she said lightly.

"No wonder you said there's nothing on earth that could make you want to get married again."

Except you—if you want me, Derek. But she couldn't say it.

"I don't blame you," he said. "After something like that…" His fist clenched. "But dammit, Macey, I'm not Jack."

She managed to say, "I think you've made that abundantly clear."

"Good. We've got that much settled. I can't quit now. I *won't* quit now. I am not going away, and I'm not taking no for an answer."

"Wait a minute. Are you proposing again?"

"Yes. Well, not exactly."

Macey's head was spinning.

"I won't push you, Macey. But there's one thing we need to get straight. Last time I told you that you could set the terms—that I would agree to any conditions you wanted to put on our marriage. But now…" He took a deep breath. "I'm willing to wait till you're ready. I'm willing to prove myself, however you think I can do that. But when you marry me, it needs to be with your whole heart. No games. No conditions."

She felt as if she was melting inside. "*When* I marry you? Not *if?*"

"When," he said firmly. "Because I won't let myself believe anything else."

She put her hands against his chest, as tentatively as if she'd never touched him before. As if he might fade away under her touch. "There's nothing you need to prove, Derek."

He looked at her for a long moment, and then pulled her close and kissed her as if he would never stop. There was nothing teasing about this caress, nothing playful. He was almost solemn, and every fiber of Macey's body responded in trust.

"I couldn't marry you then," she said finally, breathlessly. "Not when it was only for show. I was a surplus wife once, Derek—handy to have, convenient, but not exactly necessary. I couldn't live like that again. I couldn't bear it."

"You are anything but convenient," he said, punctuating his words with kisses. "You're not handy, you're a nuisance. You're a thorn in my side. You're the voice of conscience and reason and doom. And you're absolutely necessary, if I'm ever going to be happy. You'll marry me?"

"I don't play golf," she pointed out. "I wear funky earrings. And I have a frivolous name that I'm not about to change."

"Macey McConnell," he said thoughtfully. "It has a nice ring to it. I'll get used to the earrings, and I'm not all that wild about golf myself. Answer me, Macey."

"Maybe I'd better flip a coin," she said, "just to test how I feel."

He held her a few inches away. "I haven't got a quarter on me. But I have a better idea. If you want to know how you feel, I'll kiss you till you figure it out."

"Just try it and see what happens," she threatened— and then she laughed and threw her arms around his neck, and surrendered all control.

Your opinion is important to us! Please take a few moments to share your thoughts with us about your experiences with Harlequin and Silhouette books. Your comments will be very useful in ensuring that we deliver books you love to read.
***Please take a few minutes to complete the questionnaire,
then send it to us at the address below.***

Send your completed questionnaires to:
Harlequin/Silhouette Reader Survey, P.O. Box 9046, Buffalo, NY 14269-9046

---

1. As you may know, there are many different lines under the Harlequin and Silhouette brands. Each of the lines is listed below. Please check the box that most represents your reading habit for each line.

Line	Currently read this line	Do not read this line	Not sure if I read this line
Harlequin American Romance	❑	❑	❑
Harlequin Duets	❑	❑	❑
Harlequin Romance	❑	❑	❑
Harlequin Historicals	❑	❑	❑
Harlequin Superromance	❑	❑	❑
Harlequin Intrigue	❑	❑	❑
Harlequin Presents	❑	❑	❑
Harlequin Temptation	❑	❑	❑
Harlequin Blaze	❑	❑	❑
Silhouette Special Edition	❑	❑	❑
Silhouette Romance	❑	❑	❑
Silhouette Intimate Moments	❑	❑	❑
Silhouette Desiré	❑	❑	❑

2. Which of the following best describes why you bought *this book?* One answer only, please.

the picture on the cover	❑	the title	❑
the author	❑	the line is one I read often	❑
part of a miniseries	❑	saw an ad in another book	❑
saw an ad in a magazine/newsletter	❑	a friend told me about it	❑
I borrowed/was given this book	❑	other: _____	❑

3. Where did you buy *this book?* One answer only, please.

at Barnes & Noble	❑	at a grocery store	❑
at Waldenbooks	❑	at a drugstore	❑
at Borders	❑	on eHarlequin.com Web site	❑
at another bookstore	❑	from another Web site	❑
at Wal-Mart	❑	Harlequin/Silhouette Reader	❑
at Target	❑	Service/through the mail	
at Kmart	❑	used books from anywhere	❑
at another department store or mass merchandiser	❑	I borrowed/was given this book	❑

4. On average, how many Harlequin and Silhouette books do you buy at one time?

I buy _____ books at one time ❑
I rarely buy a book ❑

MRQ403HR-1A

5. How many times per month do you shop for any *Harlequin and/or Silhouette* books? One answer only, please.

1 or more times a week	❏	a few times per year	❏
1 to 3 times per month	❏	less often than once a year	❏
1 to 2 times every 3 months	❏	never	❏

6. When you think of your ideal heroine, which *one* statement describes her the best? One answer only, please.

She's a woman who is strong-willed	❏	She's a desirable woman	❏
She's a woman who is needed by others	❏	She's a powerful woman	❏
She's a woman who is taken care of	❏	She's a passionate woman	❏
She's an adventurous woman	❏	She's a sensitive woman	❏

7. The following statements describe types or genres of books that you may be interested in reading. Pick *up to 2 types* of books that you are most interested in.

I like to read about truly romantic relationships ❏
I like to read stories that are sexy romances ❏
I like to read romantic comedies ❏
I like to read a romantic mystery/suspense ❏
I like to read about romantic adventures ❏
I like to read romance stories that involve family ❏
I like to read about a romance in times or places that I have never seen ❏
Other: _____ ❏

The following questions help us to group your answers with those readers who are similar to you. Your answers will remain confidential.

8. Please record your year of birth below.
19 _____

9. What is your marital status?
single ❏ married ❏ common-law ❏ widowed ❏
divorced/separated ❏

10. Do you have children 18 years of age or younger currently living at home?
yes ❏ no ❏

11. Which of the following best describes your employment status?
employed full-time or part-time ❏ homemaker ❏ student ❏
retired ❏ unemployed ❏

12. Do you have access to the Internet from either home or work?
yes ❏ no ❏

13. Have you ever visited eHarlequin.com?
yes ❏ no ❏

14. What state do you live in?
_____

15. Are you a member of Harlequin/Silhouette Reader Service?
yes ❏ Account # _____ no ❏ MRQ403HR-1B

An offer you can't afford to refuse!

High-valued coupons for upcoming books

**A sneak peek at Harlequin's newest line—
Harlequin Flipside™**

**Send away for a hardcover by *New York Times*
bestselling author Debbie Macomber**

How can you get all this?

Buy four Harlequin or Silhouette books during
October–December 2003, fill out the form below and send
the form and four proofs of purchase (cash register receipts)
to the address below.

I accept this amazing offer!
Send me a coupon booklet:

Name (PLEASE PRINT)

Address   Apt. #

City   State/Prov.   Zip/Postal Code
                                                      098 KIN DXHT

Please send this form, along with your cash register receipts
as proofs of purchase, to:

In the U.S.:
Harlequin Coupon Booklet Offer, P.O. Box 9071, Buffalo, NY 14269-9071

In Canada:
Harlequin Coupon Booklet Offer, P.O. Box 609, Fort Erie, Ontario L2A 5X3

Allow 4–6 weeks for delivery. Offer expires December 31, 2003.
Offer good only while quantities last.

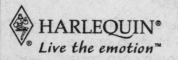

HARLEQUIN®
Live the emotion™

Silhouette®
Where love comes alive™

Visit us at www.eHarlequin.com

Q42003